TWILIGHT OF THE EASTERN GODS

Born in 1936, **Ismail Kadare** is Albania's best-known poet and novelist. Translations of his novels have appeared in more than forty countries. In 2005 he was awarded the first Man Booker International Prize for 'a body of work written by an author who has had a truly global impact'. He is the recipient of the highly prestigious 2009 Principe de Asturias de las Letras in Spain.

David Bellos is director of the Program in Translation at Princeton University and the author of *Is That A Fish in Your Ear? The Amazing Adventure of Translation*. He won the French-American Foundation's Translation Prize for his version of Georges Perec's *Life A User's Manual*, and the Goncourt Prize for Biography for *Georges Perec. A Life in Words*. He has translated seven of Ismail Kadare's novels as well as works by Romain Gary, Georges Simenon, Daniel Anselme and Georges Perec.

Praise for Ismail Kadare

'There are very few writers alive today with the depth, power and resonance of this remarkable novelist'
Herald

'One of the most important voices in literature today'
Metro

'A writer whose stark, memorable prose imprints itself on the reader's consciousness'
Los Angeles Times

'A great writer, by any nation's standards'
Financial Times

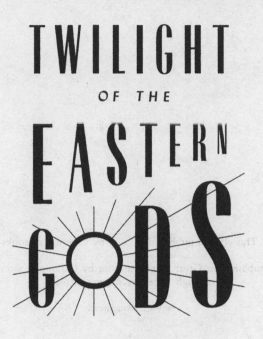

TWILIGHT OF THE EASTERN GODS

ISMAIL KADARE

Translated from the French of Jusuf Vrioni
by David Bellos

Introduction by David Bellos

CANONGATE
Edinburgh · London

This edition published in 2015 by Canongate Books

First published in Great Britain in 2014 by Canongate Books Ltd,
14 High Street, Edinburgh EH1 1TE

www.canongate.tv

1

British Library Cataloguing-in-Publication Data
A catalogue record for this book is available on
request from the British Library

ISBN 978 0 85786 619 6

Typeset in Bembo by Palimpsest Book Production Ltd,
Falkirk, Stirlingshire

Printed and bound in Great Britain by Clays Ltd, St Ives plc.

INTRODUCTION

Ismail Kadare was born in 1936 in the fortress-city of Gjirokastër, in the southernmost part of Albania. He began writing poetry in his teens and acquired a national reputation while still a university student in Tirana. At the end of his course he was selected to pursue literary studies at the Gorky Institute for World Literature in Moscow. *Twilight of the Eastern Gods* re-creates Kadare's experience of this strange 'factory of the intellect', set up to produce new generations of socialist poets, novelists and playwrights.

In many respects Kadare had a wonderful time in Moscow. For a young man newly arrived from a provincial backwater, that vast city – the cultural as well as the political hub of half the world's people – was an unending treat. Unlike tiny Tirana, it had a Metro, electric trolleybuses, neon lights, department stores, and a veritable army of pretty girls far more open to romantic encounters than puritanical Albania could offer. As a foreign student, Kadare enjoyed many privileges, including free holidays at 'residences' in the more scenic areas of the Soviet Union which were put at the disposal of its members by the Writers' Union.

But *Twilight of the Eastern Gods* does not offer a warm

or admiring reflection on the Big City where Kadare spent his two years of study abroad. It is a novel of profound disenchantment, in the tradition of Balzac's *Lost Illusions*, but with much about it that is quite particular to the privileged yet servile position of writers under Communism.

Outwardly, Kadare's Moscow years were very successful. A collection of his poetry was translated into Russian and published with a preface by the poet David Samoilov – the first of Kadare's many books to be translated into a foreign language. (Kadare gives an account of this publication in 'Truth, Secrets and Lies', a long interview published in English as an appendix to *Chronicle in Stone*.) The young Kadare also wrote his first major work in prose, a short novel titled *The City Without Signs*, the story of a literary-historical scam perpetrated by a brace of cynical and disaffected students. It was so disrespectful of political and cultural orthodoxies that Kadare did not even try to publish it until after the fall of Communism.

The inner reality was different. The professors at the Gorky Institute, the nature of the students selected for this prestigious institution, and, above all, the kind of writing that that was taught there brought Kadare to the brink of abandoning literature for good. Kadare didn't want to write about positive heroes with blond hair and jutting chins, maidens in dirndls setting out to upturn virgin soil, heroes of the Great Patriotic War or dreamy birch groves shading an idyllic collective farm*. In Moscow, Kadare learned to

---

* The Soviet Union's involvement in the Second World War, that began only with the German invasion of 1941, has always been known in Russia as 'The Great Patriotic War'.

scorn virtually every aspect of the doctrines of Socialist Realism. The best he ever had to say about the course he followed there was that it taught him how *not* to write. The consistently rainy, foggy, cold and gloomy climate of Kadare's later fictions can be read as a formal rejection of the obligatory optimism laid down by the doctrines of Socialist Realism.

Post-war Albania, initially closely allied with neighbouring Yugoslavia, had been a virtual dependency of the USSR since 1949, and it housed the only Soviet submarine base in the Mediterranean. By the later 1950s, however, Enver Hoxha, the Albanian dictator, had grown increasingly alarmed by Khrushchev's attempts to liberalise Soviet society, which he saw as a betrayal of Stalin's legacy. The strained relations culminated in a meeting of the world's Communist Party leaders in Moscow in October 1960, which expelled Albania from the socialist bloc. (This meeting is the subject of Kadare's grand and dramatic *Winter of Our Discontent*.) Ironically, it was this political divorce that made it possible for Kadare to write and eventually publish *Twilight of the Eastern Gods*.

Like many of Kadare's major works, *Twilight* was written in pieces and rewritten in different ways over a long period of time. Its themes first appeared in a poem, *Lora*, written in 1961; the following year he wrote a short story, 'A Summer in Dubulti', which is the basis for Chapter 1 of this novel; other chapters followed in fragments over a period of fifteen years, and it was not until 1978 that *The Twilight of the Eastern Gods* was ready to be released – and almost hidden – in a collective volume that also included *The Three Arched*

Bridge and *The Niche of Shame*. Even so, it was not really complete. It was translated into French by Jusuf Vrioni in 1981, and Kadare used this opportunity to smuggle back into the novel some of the more forthright passages about girls that had been omitted from the Albanian 'original'. This English translation has been done from the revised version in French first published in Volume 6 of Kadare's *Œuvres complètes* (Paris: Fayard, 1998.).

By the time of the first publication of *Twilight* as a book, of course, Albania, having broken off all relations with the Soviet Union long before, and having in addition already rejected its third major sponsor, China, found itself in a voluntary state of extreme isolation. The sour and searching critique of Russian literary life in *Twilight of the Eastern Gods* was therefore not politically contentious. Unless, of course, it was taken as casting indirect light on the treatment of literature in Albania itself. The censors in Tirana were either genuinely blind to this aspect of Kadare's novel, or else sufficiently wise to turn an officially blind eye.

The major public event that Ismail Kadare experienced in Moscow was the furore over the award of the Nobel Prize to Boris Pasternak. A member of an eminent pre-revolutionary family of artists and intellectuals, Pasternak had been educated in Germany and had emerged as a strikingly original poet around the time of the Russian Revolution. Unlike many of his relatives he chose not to emigrate, but pursued a career as an avant-garde writer throughout the 1920s. In the harsher atmosphere of the 1930s he devoted himself principally to translation, but also began work on an epic novel of a poet's life in the revolutionary period that would eventually become *Doctor Zhivago*. Finished in the early 1950s, *Zhivago* was turned down by the Soviet censors, but typescripts circulated among some groups of writers. The British philosopher Isaiah Berlin obtained a copy and smuggled it to Italy, where the left-wing publisher Feltrinelli brought out a translation in 1957. It was a sensation, and quickly translated into many other languages. Not a word of this was mentioned in the Soviet media until, in October 1958, the Swedish Academy announced that it had awarded the Nobel Prize for Literature to Boris Pasternak. In the Soviet Union, a vast, co-ordinated national campaign of denigration was launched against the author, forcing the now aged Pasternak to choose between declining the award and emigration. He took the first option.

The account of the Pasternak campaign given in *Twilight of the Eastern Gods* has nothing fictional about it: the discovery of a part of the typescript in the Writers' Union residence, the co-ordination of the press, radio and television campaign, the roles of specific individuals, right down to the inexplicably sudden halt – all these things really happened. (The excerpts from *Doctor Zhivago* given on page 60 were copied out of the French translation that Kadare was able to find on his later visits to Paris in the 1970s.) But it is also clear from this account of the persecution of Pasternak that Kadare could imagine finding himself in the same situation. In fact, by the late 1970s, Kadare's own eminence abroad, through translations of his novels into French, made him vulnerable inside Albania to accusations of being a Western stooge, an agent of capitalism or even a spy. Like Pasternak, Kadare did not abandon his homeland, however bizarre it had become. He certainly thought about defecting and even made quite detailed plans, but in the end his real response to the constraints of living as an international writer under a paranoid, isolationist Communist regime was to write a novel that is also a declaration of fidelity to Albania and its ancient folk culture.

That is the main reason why this comical send-up of Soviet literary culture is structured around the legend of Kostandin and Doruntine, a traditional Albanian story of fidelity to the given word. It is the main subject of Kadare's later novella, *The Ghost Rider*, where its deep connection to the idea of 'Albanianness' is made clearer. Like so many of Kadare's fictions, *Twilight of the Eastern Gods* is full of similar 'stubs' that serve as the central motifs of other stories and novels: readers will notice here what look like allusions to *The General of the Dead Army*, *The Niche of Shame*, and *The Three Arched Bridge*, but which are also in some part preliminary sketches of themes that constitute the main props and beams of Kadare's monumental, self-entwined and internally consistent oeuvre.

Twilight of the Eastern Gods is deeply rooted in Kadare's personal experience and in historical events, but it is neither an autobiography nor a work of history. The narrator is a young man very much like Ismail Kadare – he is even the author of a few lines of Kadare's verse – but he is nonetheless someone else. It is true that the real young writer had a good time with a number of Soviet girls: but none of them was called or even resembled Lida Snegina, as Elena

Kadare has been able to establish in her remarkable inves-
tigation of her husband's early correspondence. Conversely,
most of the teachers and students at the Gorky Institute
portrayed in this novel bear the names of real teachers and
students. They can all be seen in the class photograph of
the 1958–1960 cohort, which is reproduced on p. 193 of this
edition. As libel laws didn't exist in the Soviet Union or
in Albania, Kadare felt no need to change names – but his
caricatures of these variously slimy, self-serving, inauthentic,
alcoholic, ignorant and otherwise comical 'students of literature' aren't intended to be individually accurate or fair,
only to re-create in a work of literature the social and
cultural environment in which Kadare felt so ill at ease.

He was unable to maintain contact with his classmates
for many years owing to the break between Albania and
the rest of the socialist world. In the 1980s Kadare tried to
find out what had happened to them all, but learned only
that Hieronymus Stulpanc had taken his own life. In 1988,
he found Antaeus alive, well, and living in Athens.

Readers interested in these and other non-fictional characters mentioned in the novel can find basic details in the
Index of Names on pp. 187–192.

Because the Gorky Institute was an international institution, its corridors buzzed with many different tongues, and
Kadare pays considerable (and not always respectful) attention to the role that languages played in his education as a
writer. The only common language among the students
was Russian, but few of the characters in this novel speak
it natively or even very well. Perhaps for that reason, the
peculiarities of Russian grammar and pronunciation are

frequently highlighted, and several passages in the novel seem to be essays on the meaning of particular Russian words. The whole of Chapter 1, for example, could be thought of as a riff on *skuchno*, the Russian word for 'boring' – boring to a heart-rending degree, a boredom bordering on spleen; whereas Chapter 2 focuses on a different variety of sourness that in Russian is called *khandra*.

In translating this novel from Jusuf Vrioni's French translation I have sought to hear the Russian in the conversations that Kadare reproduced in Albanian, and to give this voyage into a now vanished culture rather more of the original sounds and signs than Vrioni thought appropriate in 1981, when there were still several million French Communists, many of whom knew Russian quite well. I've tried as best I can to make the speech of the cultivated but also irreverent young people in Moscow literary circles as lively as it undoubtedly was, but without using expressions and phrases that weren't in circulation in 1959. However poor my deferred rendition of an Albanian original to which I have no direct access, I think Kadare's main qualities survive: his humour and his anger, his self-critical wit, and his conviction, all the stronger for having been put to the test by his Moscow years, that real literature is, in the end, more important than anything else.

David Bellos
Princeton, February 2014

A NOTE ON PRONUNCIATION

Albanian is written in Latin characters but some letters and combinations are pronounced in a special way. The only one occurring in this novel is:

Xh makes the sound *dj* as in *bridge*

THE CYRILLIC ALPHABET

A few words and phrases are given in their original Russian forms. The thirty-two letters of the Cyrillic alphabet are pronounced roughly as follows:

А	a	П	p
Б	b	Р	r
В	v	С	s
Г	g	Т	t
Д	d	У	*u* as in lo*o*se
Е	ye	Ф	f
Ё	yo	Х	*kh* as in (Scottish) lo*ch*
Ж	*zh* as in pleasure	Ц	ts
З	z	Ч	*ch* as in *ch*urch
И	*i* as in b*ee*t	Ш	sh
Й	y	Щ	sh-ch as in fi*sh ch*owder
К	k	Э	e
Л	l	Ы	uh
М	m	Ь	[soft sign]
Н	n	Я	ya
О	o	Ю	yu

CHAPTER ONE

We played table-tennis outdoors, not far from the beach, until after midnight because even though the white nights had passed it still didn't get very dark. Those with the best eyes played last; the rest of us lounged against the wooden railing, watching the game and correcting the score. After midnight, when everyone had gone to bed, leaving their bats on the table to get drenched by a shower before dawn, I didn't know what to do with myself – I didn't feel like sleeping. I would wander for a while around the gardens of the Writers' Retreat (it used to be the estate of a Latvian baron), go as far as the fountain, which spurted from a group of stone dolphins, then track back to the 'Swedish House' and on down to the Baltic shore. The nights were very cold and quickly chilled you to the bone.

I did much the same thing almost every evening. On fine days, the mornings and afternoons went by quickly, with swimming and sunbathing, but evenings were dreary, and most of the residents were quite old. Almost all of them were VIPs, with titles galore, but that didn't stop evenings being dull, especially as I happened to be the only foreigner staying there.

As dusk drew in we would take our cameras down to the beach and set them so they were ready to snap at the moment the sun sank into the sea. The Baltic turned a slightly different colour each night, and we used to try to fix each successive sunset on film. Sometimes a couple of distant strollers along the waterline wandered into the shot. When we developed the film, they appeared as meaningless smudges in the endless vista. After dinner we got together again around the ping-pong table, and as I watched the small white ball going back and forth, I could feel my whole being adjusting to its pace. I would try, but usually fail, to pull myself back from the ball's metronome effect. Only every so often, in short, rebellious bursts, would I manage to break free from my enslavement to the little white sphere, whose jagged leaps, small diameter, and sharp, metallic noise when it hit the table almost succeeded in sending me into a trance. But at those instants when I recovered my lucidity I would jerk my head towards the shore, and every time I turned, like a sleepwalker, towards the water's edge I hoped to spy in the far distance, at long last, something different from what I had seen the day before. But the seashore at dusk was merciless. It had nothing to offer but a view it had probably been rehearsing since the dawn of time: silhouettes of couples walking slowly by. They probably came from the other residences in the vicinity, and after passing our house, they scattered in directions that seemed to me quite mysterious, towards resorts whose beaches bore the names of the little stations on the electric railway line, strange-sounding names like Dzintari, Majori and Dubulti. They were names I had previously read on perfume bottles and tubes of face cream in shop windows in other places, without imagining they might be the names of stations or holiday resorts.

Old men, who knew there was no point in trying to get to sleep, stayed on the benches until well after dark. As I walked around I could occasionally hear their whispers and coughs or, when they finally got up, the tapping of their sticks as they walked towards the 'Swedish House', where the oldest and most distinguished of the residents stayed.

I would carry on sauntering aimlessly, wondering how almost all of these old men could be famous writers and frequently the dedicatees of each other's works. Most of the children who ran around noisily in the daytime had had poems and stories dedicated to them by their parents, and you could tell that some of the youngsters had read the works in question. As for the older women, who chatted among themselves for hours every evening after dinner, I knew that quite a few were still stepping out on the pages of some books as good-looking girls in high heels, under the mask of initials such as D.V. or N. or even their first names. The men sometimes appeared beneath the disguise of initials in books written by women, but less often. As a rule, those men had stomach ailments, and in the dining room you could see they were on some special diet or other.

Some evenings I went to the post office in the hope that the line to Moscow would be open so I could call Lida Snegina. But the telephones were usually busy. You could only be sure of placing a call if you booked it a day in advance.

Lida was the young woman I had been seeing in Moscow. She'd come with me to the station on the gloomy day I'd left for Riga. Before the train departed, we paced slowly up and down on the rain-wet platform along with many other parting couples, and she'd said, with her eyes averted, that she found it difficult to go around with foreigners, especially foreigners from far-off lands. When I asked her why, she told me about a friend of hers who had got involved with a Belgian who had disappeared overnight, just like that, without even telling her he was going. Of course, she added, 'It may well be that not all foreigners are the same, but they often bolt without leaving so much as a word.' At least, that was what she'd heard people say.

I really ought to have riposted, but only a few moments remained before the train would depart, and the time available was much too short to quarrel and make up. So I had to choose between argument and appeasement. I chose the latter: I swallowed my pride, and declared that in any circumstance, and come what may, I would never slip away, like a thief in the night. I wanted to add that I came from an ancient Balkan land with grandiose legends about the given word, but the time left was disappearing fast and would barely permit a synopsis, let alone the full story of Kostandin and Doruntine's ghostly ride.

I liked to walk to the post office and back on my own. It wasn't a particularly scenic route – in fact, it was rather desolate, with only scraggy reeds, small piles of sand and plump thistles on either side. All the same, that particular path, like some women who, though not beautiful, possess a hidden charm, was conducive to my having new thoughts.

It was my second holiday at a writers' retreat and I knew most of the ropes, as well as the oddities of the inmates. The previous winter I had spent some time in Yalta. My room had been next to Paustovsky's. The lights stayed on in his room until late; we all knew he was writing his memoirs. Whenever I went out into the corridor I encountered the *starosta*, our course leader at the Institute, Ladonshchikov by name, who was forever watching the light in Paustovsky's room. Whenever he came across somebody in the hall, he would confide in them with a sigh and the beating of his breast, as if he were reporting the worst news in the world, that the aforementioned Paustovsky was bringing all the Jews back to life in his memoirs. What I remembered of Yalta was uninterrupted rain, games of billiards that I always lost, a few Tatar inscriptions, and the permanent look of jealousy on the utterly insignificant face of Ladonshchikov, despite the solemn air he wore of a man concerned for the fate of the Fatherland. I had hoped that life in the Riga retreat would be less sinister, but what I encountered were some of the people I had seen at Yalta, table-tennis instead of billiards, and intermittent rain, confirming Pushkin's *bon mot* about northern summers being caricatures of southern ones. The similarity of faces, conversations and names (the only ones missing were Paustovsky and Ladonshchikov, oddly enough) gave me a sense of constant *déjà vu*. The life we led there had something sterile about it, like an extract in an anthology. At Yalta, in this rather odd world, I was aware of leading a hybrid existence, where life and death were mixed up and overlapping, as in the ancient Balkan legend I hadn't

managed to recite to Lida Snegina. The idea was imposed
on me by the equation I could not help making automatically between the people around me and their doubles
– the characters of novels and plays I knew well. An irre-
pressible and somewhat diabolical desire to compare their
words, gestures and even their faces to those of their ori-
ginals had arisen the previous winter in Yalta, where for
the first time I realised that most contemporary Soviet
writers virtually never talked about money in their works.
It was like a sign. Now, in Riga, I was learning that alongside money there were many other things they did not
mention, and reciprocally, many of the topics that filled
whole chapters or acts of their works barely impinged on
their real lives. The contrast made me constantly uneasy.
Besides, there was something abnormal about being cut off
from the world like that, and it brought to mind the
monstrous beings I had seen preserved in glass jars in the
Natural History Museum.

I'd tried a few times to break away from this frozen
landscape, which seemed to me more and more like some
kind of obsolete monument, but all my efforts came to
nothing and brought me back to billiards in Yalta, then to
ping-pong at the Riga retreat. In both settings, at the weighty
winter billiards and the flimsy summer ping-pong, I only
ever lost.

It was Saturday. As always we were playing in the dim
but sufficient light of the evening, and although I was
cheered at the prospect of winning the third set after losing
the first two, I felt beside me a presence that was both new
and familiar.

It was a kind of ash-blonde smudge that reminded me of Lida's hair. The impression was so strong that I put off turning as if I wanted to give the stranger enough time to become Lida. In that brief moment I realised that, without knowing it, I had long been yearning for her to come through the sky and across the steppe, as silently as the setting of the moon, to be beside me at the table-tennis table.

The little ping-pong ball, with its irritating rebound, scraped my right ear, and as I bent down to pick it up I stole a glance at the visitor, who'd not been seen before in the gardens of our writers' retreat.

She had come up quietly and stopped amid the keen observers of the table-tennis matches, the people who put the score right when others got it wrong. Let me not make some ridiculous gesture, I thought, since the match seemed to have turned against me irrevocably. The silent ash-blonde smudge among the noisy spectators held me in its sway.

I dropped and abandoned my bat in disgust. Though I was cross I went towards the stranger and wiped my brow with a handkerchief. I was annoyed at losing three games in a row and I had a feeling someone had fiddled the score. As I wiped my face, I looked at her: she had her hands in her trouser pockets and was gazing at the table with a supercilious pout.

Night had fallen some time ago, and at the water's edge the strollers, as if they had lost their faces, had now turned into outlines, but we knew they were the people we had caught on our film an hour earlier.

My annoyance subsided and I looked more attentively at the wonderful hair of the young newcomer. In this part

of the world hair like hers was not uncommon. Sometimes
it reminded you of autumn sadness: it was, so to speak, not
of this world; it was as if its owner had come from the
moon. But this girl's hair reminded me especially of Lida.
One of my Yalta colleagues had tried to persuade me that
there was a kind of dog that reacted to such hair with
stifled yelping, as if it was greeting the full moon out on
the steppe. Subsequently, when I thought back on those
words, I became convinced that, however absurd such tall
tales might seem, they contained a grain of truth. Obviously
it wasn't referring to real dogs howling, but to humans. My
Yalta colleague must surely have gone through something
like that himself. But it couldn't be a matter of screaming
out loud, it must have been more like a silent, internal yell,
arising from an infinite quivering that was on the point of
turning into − why not? − a symphony.

'Are you having a dance here tonight?' the young woman
suddenly asked, with a lively turn of her head.

She had beautiful, serious grey eyes.

'There are never any dances here,' I replied.

She smiled tentatively. 'Why not?'

I shrugged. 'I don't know. All we have here is fame.'

She laughed, her eyes on the table, and I was pleased
with my witticism, which, though entirely unoriginal,
seemed to have had some effect. I'd heard it the day I
arrived, from the mouth of a taxi driver, whose licence-plate
number had remained fixed in my memory, like so many
other superfluous things.

'Are you from abroad?' the girl asked again.

'Yes.'

She stared at me curiously. 'Your accent gives you away,' she said. 'I don't speak perfect Russian myself, but I can tell a foreign accent.' She told me that she'd been among her own folk forty-eight hours before; that she was staying in a villa right beside our retreat; and that she was bored. However, she seemed surprised when I confided that I came from a distant country and was therefore much more bored than she was. She had never set eyes on an Albanian before. What was more, she had always imagined they were darker than Georgians, that they all had hooked noses and were keen on the kind of Oriental chanting she hated.

'Wherever did you get those ideas?' I asked rather crossly.

'I don't know. I think it's an impression I got from the exhibition you held last year at Riga.'

'Hm,' I muttered. I wanted to drop the subject.

I'd noticed more than once that ordinary Soviet citizens were much given to comparing foreigners from other socialist countries to the natives of their own sixteen republics. If you were very blond, they would say you were like a Lithuanian or an Estonian; if you had a curved nose they would think you had a Georgian look; if you had sad eyes, you must be Armenian, and so on. Some even thought that Turkey was a province of Azerbaijan that had been left on the wrong side of the border by a quirk of history. And on one sad afternoon a tipsy Belarusian tried to convince me that Armenians were really Muslims: they pretended to be Christians only to enrage the Azeris, and it was high time to sort things out down there . . .

'Have you been to Riga?' she asked me. 'What did you think of it?'

I told her I liked that sort of town.

'Isn't it too grey for you?'

I nodded.

'And what are your cities like?'

'White,' I replied, without thinking.

'That's odd,' she said. 'I've always dreamed of seeing white cities.'

I could easily have told her our towns were blue – as I once had to a gullible Ukrainian girl at Yalta last winter – but she was too attractive, and I was beginning to watch my step. She was listening to me with an odd expression, half attentive and half haughty, as she stared blankly into the distance with a smile that seemed to be a response to something happening at least twenty metres away.

We chatted for quite some time, leaning on the wooden balustrade, while the others created a commotion around the ping-pong table, getting the score wrong and squabbling over it, as if the stake really mattered.

'Do you see that fat lady with a shawl, talking angrily to her son over there?' I said.

'The one with grey hair?'

'Yes. She's the dedicatee of the famous poem that begins "When sunsets were blue, quite blue . . ."'

'Really? And how do you know?'

I told her where I had got the information. But instead of being glad in the slightest degree to pick up a morsel of literary gossip, she pouted. 'Why did you tell me that with a sort of satisfaction, almost cynically?'

'Cynically?' I protested. To be honest, I'd been glad that the old lady had provided me with a topic of conversation, but never had I thought I would be accused of gloating over a woman's ageing.

My first instinct was for self-justification, but then I thought that, in cases of this kind, attempts at explanation can only give rise to yet more misunderstandings. So I decided to say nothing.

Her face had resumed its expression of supercilious indifference.

We said nothing for several minutes, and as time ticked by we were steadily and very rapidly becoming strangers once again.

Damn that fat old woman! I thought. Why ever did she cross my path? Now this girl is going to go away and she'll leave without even saying goodnight. And I really don't want her to leave! Half an hour ago I hadn't even known she existed, but now her departure would be like an eclipse of the moon. I didn't understand why I felt so anxious, but it was undoubtedly connected to the wearisome sameness of vacation days spent among initialled individuals dotted around like statues on plinths, and with the spiritual disarray I had been suffering for some time. At last a living being had turned up in the museum! What was more, the visitor's hair and smooth neck were amazingly reminiscent of Lida Snegina's.

The ping-pong ball bounced around like a little devil and its weightless vacuity obliterated all possibility of thought. Silence between us persisted beyond endurance and I repeated in my mind: There it is! She's going to leave and I'll be all alone in this archive dump.

But she didn't go. She carried on watching the table-tennis, with distance and disdain. The light reflected by her

ash-blonde hair continued to fall on me, like an accidental
sunset, and my mind wandered back to the howls or,
rather, to the canine symphony I'd been told about in
Yalta last winter. At one point I was tempted to drop her
there and then, but I thought better of it: women in those
parts were like that and, anyway, compared to easy-going
Moscow women, girls from anywhere else in the world
seem sour.

'Shall we go for a walk?' I asked bluntly.

'Where to?' she answered, without turning her head.

'That way. Maybe there's somewhere further on that we
can dance.'

She didn't reply but started walking towards the shore.
I followed her. Sand scrunched beneath our feet. She still
had her hands in her pockets, and now her mauve blouse
looked black.

The sea stretched out on our left-hand side; on the right,
the black outlines of pines and, further away, rest houses
and the little stations on the electric train line were scattered about. Here and there through the trees you could
see tiny churches with spires higher than any I had seen
before. I'd been struggling for a while to find a topic of
conversation, and as I tried, I couldn't help fondly recalling
the image of the Ukrainian girl in Yalta who had not only
lapped up the most outlandish stories but responded to any
nonsense you fed her by throwing her arms gaily around
your neck.

But the silence between us grew heavier, and I had almost
lost hope of establishing a dialogue when suddenly she
asked me about Fadeyev. I couldn't have wished for a more

suitable question, and when I told her that in Moscow I passed his apartment every day she uttered an 'Ah!'

'There are a lot of rumours about his suicide,' she said, and then, after a pause, went on. 'You're from the capital and perhaps you heard more about it than we did.'

'Of course.'

In Moscow literary circles I had indeed heard a lot of talk about the suicide. I shared with her the most interesting pieces of gossip that were going around. She listened without responding. Suddenly it occurred to me to tell her about Fadeyev's treatment in the Kremlin hospital. It was a sad story I'd heard one evening after dinner in a Moscow suburb. It was the writer's very last attempt at getting cured. The method was to have him imbibe vodka in increasing doses day by day until his whole organism rejected it in disgust. Every morning, in the silent corridors of the hospital, there could be seen a man of considerable height dressed in an inmate's gown moving along like a sleepwalker, with unfocused eyes and unfocused mind, blind drunk, mistaking doors for people and people for objects. In little groups, hiding at the ends of the corridor or behind the doors, nurses whispered, 'Today we gave him three hundred cl, tomorrow we'll increase the dose,' and they watched him with curiosity. Some felt sorry for the man; others felt the satisfaction of ordinary people when they see a great man brought low; they were really curious to see the pride of Soviet literature turned into an unrecognisable wreck, his skull now filled with nothing but alcoholic haze.

I tried to make my story as true to life as possible and thought I had succeeded because when I finished my legs were as wobbly as if I were drunk too. She put her arm in mine and leaned on me ever so slightly.

'But why? Why?' she asked softly.

I was expecting the question and answered, with a shrug, that I had no idea. Yes, indeed, why in spite of everything had he killed himself the day after his discharge?

We walked on for a long time without saying anything. I felt my mind going numb. It had wandered back once more to the folk ballad with its legendary horse ridden simultaneously by the Quick and the Dead.

'It's such a sad story,' she said. 'Let's change the subject.'

I nodded agreement and we put an end to the conversation. We remembered we were looking for a place where there was music, then realised we had wandered a long way from my residence. The empty beach stretched for ever beside the water where, from time to time, something seemed to be stirring in the darkness. It was the flickering phosphorescence of the waves. On our other side, through the pines, we could see shapes that were white and oblong, like stone belfries. A train whistled somewhere in the distance. My mind went back to Lida seeing me off on the train at Rizhsky Voksal, the Moscow terminus, and to the legend I'd not managed to recite to her.

'A penny for your thoughts?' she asked.

'Have you read Bürger's "Lenore"?' I enquired abruptly. She shook her head.

'And Zhukovsky's "Ludmila"?'

'Oh, yes. We studied it at school!'

'It's the same story,' I told her. 'Zhukovsky just translated Bürger's version.'

'I remember vaguely our teacher telling us about that,' she said. 'Although Russians don't like to mention that sort of thing.'

She had no great sympathy for Russians and barely hid it.

'But Bürger didn't make anything up either,' I went on. 'He borrowed the story from others as well and, like Zhukovsky, distorted it.'

'Bürger was German, wasn't he?'

'Yes.'

'Who did he borrow it from?'

I opened my mouth to say, 'From us,' but held back so I did not resemble those spokesmen for small nations who are forever intent on saying 'we' or 'our people' with the kind of pride or bluster that makes my heart sink, because even they barely believe what they are saying.

I was cautious about what I had to say next. I explained that the Balkan Peninsula, even though more or less everyone – even the Eskimos! – detests it, was, whether it ruffled you or not, the home of outstanding poetry, the birthplace of many legends and ballads of incomparable beauty. It was one of those, the legend of Death who rises from his grave to keep his word, that had inspired Bürger to write 'Lenore', though he had made a pretty dismal job of it. I added that all the Balkan peoples had invented variations on the legend. She should not take me for a chauvinist, but our own version was the most moving and therefore the most beautiful. Even a Greek poet who was on my course in Moscow had agreed with me on that.

'I believe you,' she said. 'Why might I think the Greek version better?'

'Because of Homer,' I said. 'Because he belongs to them.'

'You're right,' she said. 'But please tell me what the legend says!'

I was expecting her to ask for it. Straight away! I thought. You'll get to hear it right now! It seemed I just had to tell the story that summer, come what may. If I'd not managed to do it at the station when I was saying farewell to Lida Snegina, it was probably because my brain hadn't yet processed it well enough to enable me to restore it to perfection. But I felt that the moment had now come. I took a deep breath, summoned my skill with words, concentrated my energy, and launched into an explanation of what it meant for an Albanian mother of nine to marry her only daughter to a man from a faraway place 'over the seven mountains'. I sensed that my companion was listening to me, but also that the Baltic, that body of foreign water, was helping me along as it lapped that northern shore. The mother didn't want her daughter to marry so far away, since she knew the girl would never be able to come home for a family wedding or funeral. But her youngest son, Kostandin, made a promise that, whatever came to pass, he would set out and bring his sister home, however far he had to go. So, the mother gave her approval and married Doruntine to a foreign knight. Alas, a harsh winter soon came, with a bloody war; all nine sons fell in battle and the mother was left alone with her grief.

'I don't remember any of that!' my listener exclaimed.

'Of course not. They cut it all out!' I said, in a menacing tone, as if Bürger and Zhukovsky were horse thieves.

She couldn't take her eyes off me now.

'Kostandin's grave was nothing but mud,' I went on, 'because he had broken the *besa*. In our land a promise is sacred, and breaking it is the deepest shame that can befall anyone. Do you understand? It's said that if even an oak tree betrays a secret, its branches will wither and die.'

'How enchanting!' she cried.

I went on with my story. One Sunday the mother went as she usually did to visit the nine graves of her sons, lit a candle for the first eight and two candles for her youngest. Then she called to Kostandin: 'Kostandin, have you forgotten the promise you made to bring my daughter back if there should be a wedding or a funeral?' And then she did something that Albanian mothers do very rarely indeed: she cursed her dead son. 'O you who have failed to keep your word, may the earth disgorge you!' And when night fell . . .

Scarcely had I uttered those words than my companion grasped my hand and exclaimed, 'How terrible!' Then, after a pause, as if she wanted to bring the conversation down to earth, she pointed out that none of what I had just told her was to be found in ballads in this part of the world.

'Don't mention those thieves to me ever again!' I blurted out almost angrily. 'So, when the night was deep and the graveyard lit by the moon, the lid of Kostandin's tomb rose, and from the grave, his face quite white and his hair a muddy tangle, the Dead Man cursed by his mother came.'

Her hand was shaking but, regardless, I went on, 'Kostandin rose from his grave, because, as it is said in our land, the given word makes Death step back . . . Do you understand?'

The quivering had moved up from her hands to her shoulders, so I told her then about Kostandin's moonlit ride to the far country where his sister had married. The young man found Doruntine in the middle of a feast and hoisted her onto his horse to take her back to her mother. On the way she kept asking, 'Brother, why are you so pale? Why do you have mud in your hair?' And he replied every time: 'It's from weariness and the dirt of the road.' They rode on together on the horse, the Dead Man and the Living Girl, until they got to the village where their mother lived. Kostandin brought the horse to a standstill outside the church. Behind the surrounding wall, with its iron gate, the church was almost entirely dark. Only the nave was faintly lit. Kostandin said to his sister, 'You go on. I have something to do here.' He pushed open the iron gate and went into the graveyard, never to emerge from it again.

I stopped.

'How gripping!' she said.

'Did you really like that version of the legend?' I asked.

'Yes, a lot. It's so different from the one we learned at school!'

'So don't mention those wretches to me again!'

We had walked quite a distance as I told the tale and now we could hear a band.

I felt astonishingly unburdened by having at last told the story of Kostandin and Doruntine. As I was glad she had liked it, I was tempted to tell her the other great Albanian legend, the one about the man who was buried alive in the pillar of a bridge, but I held back for fear of overdoing the folklore.

We were walking towards the source of the music and soon we found ourselves in front of a restaurant's illuminated sign.

'The Lido,' I read aloud. 'Shall we go in?'

'Wait', she said. 'It must be expensive. And I don't like the look of it.'

I stuck my hands into my pockets and pulled out all the change I had. 'I've got a hundred and ten roubles. Maybe that'll be enough.'

'No, no. I really don't like the look of this place. Let's go somewhere else.'

I knew my resources wouldn't be adequate for the Lido, so I didn't insist.

Further on we heard more music. We wandered towards another place where a dance night had been organised by the veterans' and workers' holiday resorts. Nobody stopped us at the door. We went in. People were dancing. Others sat drinking at tables set around the dance floor. In the lamplight my companion looked even prettier and we found nothing better to do than to dance. There was a lot of noise. Now and again customers who were drunk were shown the door. In an environment where we were both outsiders, we felt closer to each other. She was serious yet casual, which I liked. We went up to the bar and ordered two brandies. She had style, and drank with confident movements. At a nearby table three middle-aged men were talking in Latvian. They looked at us inquisitively, and one of them, the oldest, asked my companion a question. I didn't understand a word of the language, but I grasped that he wanted to know what nationality we were. Obviously they'd guessed I was a foreigner, and when she answered them, they showed some interest, smiled at me, and one got up to fetch two more chairs.

So, we made their acquaintance. They were veterans of the Russian Revolution, and we started a conversation, my girlfriend acting as interpreter. All three seemed relatively well informed about Albania but they had never met an Albanian before. They kept repeating that they were very happy to have the opportunity of meeting me. I was pleased that at least they didn't imagine every Albanian had a bulbous nose and a Zapata moustache. However, for some reason they thought we were all plump and round, which my own figure certainly did not bear out.

'Are you two engaged?' the oldest of them asked.

We shook our heads, then looked at each other, and from that point on she seemed even closer to me, for we were now connected by a small secret, our first, that these three men didn't know we had only just met or that we were still using the formal вы to say 'you' to each other.

They'd been soldiers in a Latvian regiment that had had the task of defending the Kremlin after the Revolution. I'd heard a lot about the 'Latvian Guards', as they were called. A few days before, I'd seen the impressive cemetery in Riga, with its hundreds of graves laid out in straight lines beneath a huge fresco showing Nordic horses and horsemen leaning over the dead. It hadn't occurred to me then that I would ever meet survivors of that regiment, let alone sit down at their table with a girl and share a drink.

Now and then they spoke to me in Russian, but it was very odd Russian. I guessed if you learned a language in a fortress of the Bolshevik Revolution, subjected to alerts and White Russian plots, kept at your post by hatred of the old regime, it was bound to turn out rather strangely.

'Did you know,' one asked, 'that near here, on the Riga coast, at Kemeri, if memory serves me right, one of your kings bought a villa and lived in it for a few months?'

'An Albanian monarch?'

'Yes, that's right,' he said. 'I remember reading it in a newspaper, in 1939 or 1940, I think.'

'We've only ever had one king,' I said. 'He was called Zog.'

'I don't recall the name, but I remember very well that he was King of Albania.'

'How odd,' I said, feeling the irritation that arises when you bump into a tiresome acquaintance in some foreign land. His two friends were also aware that an Albanian royal had bought a beach villa at Kemeri. The girl's curiosity was aroused and she began talking to them excitedly.

'Oh! So it's true!' she said, clapping her hands. 'How interesting!'

For the first time that night I thought I saw her face go dreamy, and I scowled. Ahmet Zog, I said inwardly, why did you have to come all this way to mess things up for me?

'Are you upset?' she asked. 'Does it annoy you to know that he came here?'

'Oh! I don't really care. I never had much interest in him anyway!'

'Well, well. You're full of yourself, aren't you?' she riposted.

Oh dear! I thought. Now she thinks I'm jealous of the old king. To be honest, I had felt slightly jarred when her eyes, which had been grey and serious up to that point, had lit up at the mention of the former sovereign. I tried to hide my feelings from her by addressing myself mainly to the three veterans: 'He must have come here after he fled. He had a lot of enemies and was very cautious. Maybe he thought this was far enough away from Albania.'

'Oh, yes, it is a long way,' one man said.

If only this conversation were over, I thought. We raised our glasses and toasted each of us in turn, starting with my girlfriend. They were tipsy. They said they would like to see us dance, and as we moved around the floor they watched us with kindly eyes and smiled at us from time to time.

My girlfriend realised how late it was and said we should leave. We had a last drink with the three Latvians. Then, as we were preparing to go the veterans put their heads together and, apparently in my honour, began to sing very softly '*Avanti popolo*'. There was a lot of noise, and they were singing softly in their slightly hoarse baritone voices. Maybe they thought it was an Albanian song, or perhaps they knew it was Italian but sang it anyway, because I came from a faraway country next door to where the song was from, or perhaps it was the only foreign song they knew and they were singing it simply because I was a foreigner. I refrained from filling them in, and didn't ask them to explain, because none of it mattered, but I stayed to listen to the familiar tune and lyrics, which they mangled, except for the word *rivoluzione*, which they transformed into *revolutiones,* with the typically Latvian -*es* ending.

We bade them farewell and left. It was rather cool outside. In the dark the shoreline was barely visible. My companion put her arm in mine and we set off in a random direction, as before, except our pace was slower now and the crunching of the sand seemed louder in the deeper silence all around. We walked on without speaking, and it occurred to me that we had now turned into one of the silhouettes that at the writers' retreat we captured in our snapshots of the sunset.

'Where are we going?' she asked.

'I don't know. Wherever you want.'

'I prefer not to know where I'm going. I like walking aimlessly, like this.'

I told her I also liked wandering with no destination in mind. Then we fell silent and could again hear the dull crunch of our footfalls on the sand. We didn't know which way we were going. It wouldn't have been hard to find our bearings and make our way towards our respective lodgings, but it amused us not to do so and, as it turned out, we were going in the opposite direction.

'Apart from your king, have any other Albanians come to this country on holiday?' she asked.

'I don't know. It's possible.'

'I hope not,' she said. 'I'd like you to be the only Albanian who's been here, apart from your king.'

She said the words 'apart from your king' in an intimate tone, as if the king and I were two knights-in-waiting on this deserted beach, one of whom she had deigned to favour.

'Wouldn't it be an amazing thing if you were the only two Albanians ever to have spent a holiday here?' she added, soon after.

'I can't say,' I replied. 'I wouldn't see that as particularly unlikely.'

'I see!' she said. 'You think it's more interesting to know that "When sunsets were blue" was dedicated to an old lady with a weight problem?'

I didn't know what to say and began to laugh. She was getting her own back. I've lost it, I thought. A fat lady and an ex-king must surely be enough to ruin a date. Damn you, King, why did you trip me up again?

Then, as if she had been reading my thoughts, she said: 'Do you really think I've got any sympathy for monarchs? To tell the truth, I think they're all pathetic old men destined to have their heads cut off.'

I burst out laughing again.

'Like in period films . . .' I said, but stopped for fear of upsetting her.

'What?' she asked.

'Our king was young, rough and sly, nothing like a pathetic old man.'

My words had no apparent effect on her.

'Was he good-looking?' she asked, after a while.

So that was what she wanted to know! 'No,' I said. 'He had a hooked nose and liked Oriental singing.'

'You sound like you're jealous!'

We laughed, and I admitted that the monarch had actually been a very handsome man.

'Really?' she cried, and we were laughing again. Then we stopped talking for quite a while, with her leaning on my arm, and I felt like whistling a tune. But the shadow of the ex-king fell on us, just as Fadeyev's had walked beside us earlier.

At one point we heard a muffled clatter in the distance,

then a light – maybe the headlamp of a locomotive – threw a pale beam from far away. Probably it reminded her of the legend I'd told her because she mumbled something about it. I asked her which part of my tale she'd liked most. She replied that it was the point when Kostandin stopped at the cemetery gate and said to his sister, 'You go on. I have something to do here.'

'I don't know how to explain this . . . It's something everybody might have felt in some form or another . . . Even though it doesn't seem to have any connection with reality . . . How can I say . . .'

'You mean that it expresses universal pain, like all great art?'

'"You go on. I have something to do here." Oh! It's both terrible and magnificent!'

It occurred to me again that it was perhaps the right time to tell her the other legend, the one about the man walled into the bridge.

'"You go on. I have something to do here,"' she repeated softly, as if to herself. 'Yes, it does express something like universal pain, doesn't it? As if all people on earth . . . I don't know how to put it . . . well, that everybody has their share of that pain . . . With some left over, so to speak, for the moon and the stars . . .'

We held forth for a while on the universality of great art. On reflection, I reckoned it was better not to tell her the second legend: it might weaken the impact of the first.

As we chatted about art that was great or even just ordinary, we found we had got to a small station.

'It's the last train,' she said, as we paced up and down

the empty platform, our footsteps echoing on the concrete. The imposing, almost empty green train soon pulled into the station and screeched to a halt in front of us. Perhaps it was the one whose headlamp we had seen shining in the distance. The doors opened but nobody got off. A second later, as the carriages juddered into movement again, my companion suddenly grabbed my arm and yelled, 'Come on! Let's get on!' and rushed towards a door. I followed. She was brighter now than she'd been all evening. Her eyes were aflame as we went into an empty compartment, with dim lighting that made the long bench seats seem even more deserted.

We went into the corridor and stared at the thick night through the window.

'Where are we going?' I asked.

'No idea!' she answered. 'I really don't know. All I know is that we're going somewhere!'

I didn't care where we were going either, and I was happy to be alone with her that night on an almost empty train.

'If the villa is in this direction, I'd like to get off to see the place where your king spent his holidays, at his old estate.'

I smiled, but she insisted, so I gave in to avoid a quarrel. She was almost too entrancing when she was stubborn. Anyway, there's nothing more exasperating than having a row in an enclosed space like a railway compartment, where you can't just leave your partner in the hope she'll call you back or run after you to make up, the ritual of lovers since time immemorial. I yielded, but we realised we were travelling in a direction we did not know: stations came and went at such short intervals and were so like each other that it soon became impossible to tell them apart. Nonetheless, each time the train stopped at a station we tried to make out its name in the hope it would turn out to be the one we were looking for. My companion and I remained standing in the corridor and I thought how pretty she was. There was nobody at any of the stations, and the departures and arrivals boards looked rather sad without a single traveller to look at them.

'We don't have any tickets,' I said.

'That's hardly a worry! At this time of night there's no ticket inspector.'

I began to whistle. She smiled at me. We were staring at each other, and had she not also glanced at the station names we would have missed ours. Suddenly she clapped her hands and shouted a name. The train stopped and we jumped out. A few seconds later it moved off again, rattling away into the black night. Silence fell once more on the deserted platform where we stood alone.

'So, we did get on the right train, after all,' she said, pointing to the sign with the station's name.

'Makes no difference to me!' I said. That's true, I thought. Evenings at the residence are so mortally dull that the further away I can get, the happier I shall be.

'It does to me,' she retorted. 'I want to see your king's villa.'

'How are we going to find it?' I asked

'I don't know. But I think we'll manage.'

We crossed the tracks and walked towards the beach.

Again she put her arm in mine and I felt the weight of her body. The beach was entirely empty. Through the darkness you could just make out the gloomy outlines of the buildings on the seafront. There were no lights on anywhere. All you could hear was the swell of the sea, which made it feel even lonelier.

We passed the locked gates and shuttered windows of silent villas, and from time to time she wondered which might have been the royal residence.

'Perhaps it's this one,' she said. 'It's more ornate and luxurious than the others.'

'Could be,' I replied. It was a large two-storey house set in a formal garden behind iron railings. 'Yes, perhaps it is,' I added. 'He was very rich and spared no expense.'

'Shall we have a rest?' she suggested.

We sat down on the stone steps, and as she'd said she was cold, I allowed my arm to wrap itself around her shoulders. I was cold too. There was a breeze coming in from the sea and strands of her hair, which were weighed down by the damp of the night, like copper filaments, occasionally brushed my face.

'What are you thinking?' she asked, impulsively using the more intimate ты form of the verb. Neither of us was a native Russian speaker, and the complex rules on how to say 'you' caught us out occasionally.

I shrugged. To be honest, there was nothing in my brain that could have been called a thought. At first I was tempted to say, 'I'm thinking of you,' but it seemed too banal.

'I know what you're thinking,' she said. 'You're thinking that maybe your king sat on these steps, that maybe he looked out at the sea just as we're doing now, and that you are perhaps the only Albanian to have come here since he did.'

'No, I'm not,' I said.

'Yes, you are!' she insisted.

'I really am not!'

'You don't want to admit it, out of pride.'

'Frankly, no,' I said once more, wearily. 'It makes no difference to me whether or not he sat on these steps. Far from stirring my imagination, as you think it does, the very idea—'

'Then you must be completely devoid of imagination!'

'Perhaps I am.'

'Please forgive me,' she said. 'I didn't mean to offend you.'

We said nothing for several minutes. Now and again I could feel her icy hair on my cheek. The arm I had round her shoulder had gone numb. It was like one of those heavy, damp branches blown down by the wind during the night that you find lying outside the house in the morning.

So we'll have to talk about the ex-king, I thought. From the moment the old interloper had been mentioned that evening I'd avoided saying anything about him, but I knew that I could put it off no longer.

I took a deep breath, feeling tired even before I began. I intended to tell her about Albania and especially its former poverty, which we'd learned about at school, where the monarch was discussed even less positively than the sultans, Nero or the tsars. I told her more or less that the Albanians who had given birth to those magnificent legends (I must have told her about the man walled into the bridge by then) were so poor that although most of them lived near the sea they had never seen it when that man (I waved at the iron railings) had been buying himself lavish properties abroad and running around with tarts on foreign beaches. I went on to tell her that Albanians were then so destitute that in some parts of the country the highlanders owned no more than a single piece of cloth they bound around their heads, like a turban; it was a shroud that they carried with them at all times so that if they happened to be killed on the road a passer-by could give them a proper burial.

I felt her fingers running up the back of my neck, as if she was searching for a shroud, and shivered.

'Had you ever heard that before?' I asked.

'No,' she said. 'I knew that Albania was a land of exquisite beauty but what you've just told me is so sad.'

She carried on running her fingers through my hair, above the nape of my neck, and after a pause she added: 'You know what? Maybe you're right where kings are concerned, but you still have to let your imagination roam sometimes . . . Indulge in a bit of fantasy. Most books nowadays are so boring, with their permanently smiling and always rugged heroes. Don't you think?'

I didn't know what to say. She was quite possibly right, but all the same I tried to remonstrate with her, saying that the Revolution had had its own beauty, such as the three Latvian Guards we'd met a couple of hours earlier, or Lenin, who had made all the kings, tsars, khans, emirs, emperors, sultans, caliphs and popes look like pygmies, like . . .

I'd let myself get carried away by the tidal wave of Lenin-worship. Encomia of that sort were common. A fellow student had told me that it was the safest way yet found to take Stalin down a notch. The two were portrayed as radically different, almost as if they had been enemies; there were even hints that Lenin had been persecuted by his successor, but that everything would be brought into the open at the right time . . .

'Yes, sure, OK,' she acknowledged, sounding tired, 'but most contemporary books about the Revolution and about Lenin are so dry and . . . I can't find the right word.'

I realised it would not be easy to contradict her.

'Perhaps it's because Shakespeare wrote about kings,' I blurted out, without thinking. Indeed, I pondered, Shakespeare wrote about kings, but the people who write about the Revolution . . . In my mind I saw in the long procession of all those mediocre writers, eyes lit with envy (some were still jealous of Mayakovsky), who had made fools of themselves in the view of the younger generation by writing so badly about the Revolution. I could see the crimson face of Vladimir Yermilov, whom I found odious because I knew he was one of those responsible for Mayakovsky's suicide. Every time I saw him, with his ugly snout, having lunch in the dining room at the writers' retreat I was astounded that the assembled company didn't charge at him, beat him up, lynch him, drag him out to the road, then to the dunes and all the way to the dolphin fountain. Once in a while I said to myself that the absence of an event of that sort must mean that something was out of kilter in the house, completely out of true.

'So I'm not entirely wrong, am I?' she said.

'What do you mean?' I was startled. My mind was in a muddle, and I didn't grasp in what sense my companion could claim to be right. Our conversation turned back to the ex-king of Albania, and it troubled me that she could cling to any illusions about him. I intended to describe the squalor of his court, with all its princes and princesses, the highnesses' aunts and uncles, and the cohorts of courtiers, whose grotesque portraits I had so often seen in old magazines when I was doing research for my dissertation in the National Library. But it was too late to start a conversation of that kind, so I said nothing.

Maybe it was my not saying anything, or the way my arm round her shoulders stiffened, that made me think she'd read my thoughts, because she suddenly whispered: 'Perhaps it's not his villa anyway.'

'Could be.' I gave a deep sigh. I was worn out by this Pyrrhic victory, because I was angry with the ex-king – very angry, in fact – for having loomed up out of the past to spoil my night out. Then it occurred to me that no evening is ever entirely safe, and you can never know in advance from which forgotten depths the attack will come. But then I thought that it was perhaps no coincidence that the ex-king's ghost had cropped up when I'd been depressed, and in this place, on deserted dunes where the dead and the living team up in pairs to ride on the horses of legend.

'What's your name?' she asked, after a protracted silence.

I told her, and she leaned forward to trace my initials with her finger on the smooth wet sand.

I don't know why but my mind turned to the initials

of the fat woman, and then to the length of the evening that had now become a whole night, just as a girl turns into a woman. In a minute we would stand up and leave to walk in the darkness alongside the rail tracks so we wouldn't get lost. Then I imagined I would walk her back to her villa, that I would kiss her and that she would slip away without even saying goodnight, and that I wouldn't take offence since I knew that was what local girls usually did after the first kiss. Tomorrow she'd come back to where we would be playing ping-pong and still be arguing over the score, and then we would go for a walk at sunset, along the waterline, exactly when the shutter-fiends would be focusing their cameras to catch it. We would slowly turn into black-and-white silhouettes and the shallow water would bounce our image back, like a catapult, to annoy people looking in frozen solitude at the far horizon. Then, like most of the silhouettes that sauntered along the shore in the evening, we would enter a dark space inside unknown cameras, and, later, when the films came to be developed, we would re-emerge from the Nordic dusk in the snapshots of strangers, not one of whom would know who we were or what we'd been doing there.

'It's very late,' she said. 'We ought to get back.'

Yes, we really should. We stood up without a word and moved off in the direction we had come from, passing in front of silent front doors with metal knockers shaped like human hands. For some reason I always imagined that crimes must be committed behind doors with that kind of knocker or behind the railings that enclosed silent gardens. At this time of night there were no trains. She said we would have to go as far as the main road to find a taxi or a passing car. We got to the highway, but there was not much traffic and, as usually happens in such circumstances, none of the vehicles that stopped was going in our direction. At long last an aged couple on their way home from a silver-wedding celebration gave us a lift to one of the stations — I had read its name on bottles of nail-varnish and shampoo. From there, we walked.

We got back to Dubulti before daybreak. Our conversation had become intermittent perhaps because our minds were also losing clarity, as if our thoughts had been transported into the ionosphere. I escorted my companion to her door, and what I had expected came to pass. As I moved off I turned back once more and saw a hazy glow coming from one of the villa's windows, giving it a platinum sheen. I recalled the desire to scream that my comrade had spoken of last winter in Yalta, and it occurred to me that the similarity of the sounds in *platinum* and *planet* was not entirely coincidental. I'd had direct confirmation of that when my companion had started running, just as Lida had run away in Neglinnaya Street, with the same strange and almost astral aura over her head.

I'll tell you my ballad, too, as soon as I'm back in Moscow, I thought, as I crossed the formal gardens on my way back to the guesthouse. I felt as if the shape and weight of my limbs had altered, as if I was walking on the moon. As I went past the dew-drenched ping-pong table, with its two bats casually abandoned on it after the last game, I reflected that a man can encounter more marvels in a single night than his anthropoid forebears got to see in tens of thousands of years of evolution. I went past the fountain with the dolphin sculptures, where I should have slain Yermilov long ago. Now I was walking past the chalets. All were dark and silent, and I had an urge to shout, 'Wake up, Shakespeares of the Revolution!' I was just going past the 'Swedish House', where the most eminent writers were staying, when the sound of coughing broke the lonely silence. I stood still. Those were old lungs coughing: a cough with a procession of croaks and sighs in its wake.

As I followed the path that led to my chalet I turned one last time and gazed on the unending vista of dunes that a thin northern light was beginning to whiten. Something would not let me take my eyes off the scene. Somewhere out there lay strewn the bones of the horses on whose backs we had ridden just a few hours before in the company of the dead. What a long night that was! I thought, and, half asleep, I wended my way to bed.

CHAPTER TWO

Our train came into Moscow in the twilight. It was a very long one. Throughout the day's journey, sunshine had alternated with heavy showers, and I imagined that some of the carriages were gleaming in the sun's last rays while others were still wet with rain. The front must now be in the bad-weather zone because I could see raindrops banging against the windows. But this time the train did not emerge into sunshine. Once we had got through the stormy patch, it seemed that night had fallen, dispelling the light of day. On the empty flat lands beyond the blackened panes, twilight and darkness fought it out in silence. The struggle was brief – the bad weather surely helped – and it was soon obvious that all along the track and well beyond it everything had now succumbed to night.

Two or three times I thought we were already in Moscow but it was the twinkling lights of outlying suburbs that tangled in my head until I shook myself free of daydreams.

Over the summer I had sometimes dreamed of Moscow: I was alighting in the capital but had lost my bearings and could not find the city centre. I would stop on a pavement; the traffic lights were out of order, and electric trolleybuses were gliding past, as great stags do in fairy tales. At Yalta, too, as in Riga, I had felt homesick for the city, and I'd gone to the rest-house library to hunt out a contemporary novel with detailed descriptions of the city where I had once lived and where I expected to spend a further period of my life. But the libraries of Yalta and Dubulti had left me wanting. Not a single Soviet novel contained anything like an exact description of Moscow. Even characters who lived there or were visiting always remained in some imaginary street, as I did in my dreams, and almost never turned into Gorky Street, Tverskoy Boulevard, Okhotny Ryad, or the environs of the Metropole Hotel, as if they were frightened of the city centre. And if they did wander into it they seemed stunned: they heard nothing and saw nothing – or, rather, they had eyes and ears only for the Kremlin and its bells. They would flee the centre, as if in panic, and I could feel their terror in the rhythm of the prose, which calmed only when the author took us away from Moscow, perhaps to his remote collective farm where he could squat cross-legged on the floor and describe in minute detail each of the alleyways and squares of his village.

I had tried without success to work out the relationship between the dull anxiety I felt in my dreams about Moscow and the way Soviet writers steered clear of the capital, as if they were sending themselves into exile.

The lights outside the windows were dancing less frantically and I guessed the train had slowed. With a whistle that seemed to run parallel to the tracks, it was pulling into Moscow's Rizhsky Voksal almost timidly beneath early autumn rain. I put my face to the windowpane hoping to catch a first glimpse of the station's lights. I sensed a muted illumination rising within me. At long last the concrete platform appeared and, from the first few feet, it looked empty. It slithered along the side of the carriage like a wet, grey snake. I guessed that Lida, to whom I'd sent a telegram a couple of days earlier, had not come to meet me. She has another boyfriend: that was my first thought. No, was the second. She'd been there a while and was waiting for the train to come to a halt before showing herself. She's got another boy— Stop it! I remembered that the engine's whistle had announced our arrival: the locomotive had been first into the station and had seen what was happening on the platform before anyone else.

'Beware the summer!' a fellow student had said to me just before we parted at the start of the holidays. 'It has a powerful hold over Russian girls . . .'

To illustrate his own summer failures, he told me several stories in which stations featured alongside tickets bearing unlucky numbers.

Another boyfriend. Or an abortion . . . I vaguely remembered that last time she'd asked me to be careful ('Just this time, only this time!') but I hadn't listened.

I stepped down onto the platform with my suitcase. Here and there, bodies entwined, with conjoined heads that resembled oversized seashells. They, too, have spent the summer apart, I thought, but they haven't forgotten each other.

I plunged into a taxi on the square outside the station and blurted out the address I wanted – Butyrsky Khutor, the Gorky Institute's student housing block – to the back of the aged driver's neck. He was wearing a fur hat.

Unlike the Institute's old two-storey house on Tverskoy Boulevard, the residential hall for undergraduate and graduate students at Butyrsky Khutor was a seven-floor hulk in off-white brick that had already lost its colour, like most recent constructions. Not knowing why, but with some apprehension, I leaned forward so I would spot it in the distance among the other buildings. My face was pressed to the window when its outline emerged and I suddenly became aware of my own anxiety. The block was almost entirely dark. I had expected to see lights on in the windows, but only one was lit, on the sixth or seventh floor, and its faint gleam underscored the air of abandonment the building gave off. I told myself that nobody was back yet from their vacation.

I settled up with the cab driver, got out and walked towards the door, looking up, as if to make doubly sure that the building really was empty. All the floors were dark, but the fourth, the women's floor, seemed particularly so.

I stopped at the porter's lodge on the ground floor. It struck me that Auntie Katya wasn't as welcoming as usual. She seemed to be searching for something in her desk drawer and it crossed my mind that a telegram, bearing bad news, might have come for me from Albania. But in her eyes, through the thick spectacle lenses, I saw not a glimmer of sympathy.

'You, my boy, and your friend, the other one from Albania,' she said, 'you're to report to the police.'

I frowned. I was about to ask her why when I saw in her face the same question: it had cancelled out her usual bonhomie. 'Why?' I asked all the same.

Lida's abortion flashed through my mind.

'I don't know. I heard them say something about your ID documents.' She pronounced *dokumenty* with the stress on the second syllable, like all uneducated Russians.

Through her circular glasses her eyes seemed to be asking: So what did you and he get up to over the summer?

'My papers are all in order,' I said. 'And my friend has already gone back to Albania.'

She shrugged her shoulders and returned to scrabbling in her desk drawer. I was expecting her to hand over a packet of letters or newspapers from Albania, but the drawer shut with a sharp click.

'Don't I have any mail?'

She shook her head.

I picked up my suitcase and turned away. The lift was out of order. And my room was on the sixth floor. I started walking up the staircase, shifting my case, which was heavy, from hand to hand, wondering why I had to report to the police.

At last I got to the door of my room, opened it and went in, leaving my case in the corridor. I was exhausted. I sat on the bed and hugged my knees. For a moment I felt that all I wanted was to lie on the bed and sleep until that joyless day had been wiped from my memory. However, a few seconds later I did exactly the opposite. I stood up and started to pace up and down. My reel-to-reel tape recorder was on the table, its lid still open from the last time I had played it with Lida. I had recorded music on the tapes, but just then it seemed easier to move the Cyclops's stone from the door of an ancient tomb and carry out its mummy than to switch on that machine. I don't know why, but the idea of listening to music in that desert seemed monstrous.

Without stopping to think what I was doing, I opened the door and went out into the corridor. It seemed longer than usual, with its single nightlight gleaming somewhere towards the other end. I stood still for a minute, my mind a blank. The corridor was truly endless: maybe sixty doors opened on to it. No corridor before had played such an important role in my life. I recalled how it looked late at night on noisy Saturdays when young drunks, slumped on the floor, mumbled lunatic verse, or tried to break down self-locking doors that had shut in their faces.

I walked slowly. The flooring, which had been damaged in places, creaked under my feet. The Corridoriad . . . I felt a quiver of the kind usually set off by a combination of good and bad memories. Five other corridors ran beneath this one, and a seventh above it, and much the same things had happened in each one: people had walked along them, gone into their rooms, come out again, had friends in, swapped literary gossip, consisting of plots and suppositions often much better constructed than their own works; they'd escorted to the lift speechless, smiling and weeping women or girls who, once behind the openwork metal door, resembled caged birds eager to fly away or wild animals stuck in a trap. Sometimes, when a girl was the first to step in, she would slam the door in the face of her companion and, while the lift made its slow descent, he would run down the stairs to catch her arrival. The stairway and the pursuer twisted round the lift shaft like a vine around a monumental column.

I walked on, the floorboards still creaking beneath my feet. The emptiness in the corridor was unbearable. That door was Ladonshchikov's. Further on I reached Taburokov's – he was from Central Asia. Then, in sequence, I passed the doors of Hieronymus Stulpanc, from Latvia, Artashez Pogosian, from Armenia, then those of the two Georgians, who were both called Shota (one was a Stalinist, the other anti), Yuri Goncharov – he was Russian – then Kyuzengesh, from the far north; he was a Yakut or maybe even an Eskimo – his face, especially his teeth, were the sad grey colour of the tundra – and spoke disjointed Russian in such a soft voice that it sounded like the rustling of reeds. Every time I encountered him I felt like a lonely wanderer about to sink into marshland. Then came the doors of A. Shogentsukov, from the Caucasus, and Maskiavicius, from Lithuania.

Students on our course filled most of the rooms on the sixth floor. No names were posted on the doors, even though most of the residents were famous writers in their home regions or towns. Some were the chairs of the Writers' Union in an Autonomous Republic or Region and had been obliged by the burdensome duties of their position or by insidious plots to give up their studies. At long last, after overcoming their adversaries, having accused them of Stalinism, liberalism, bourgeois nationalism, Russophobia, petty nationalism, Zionism, modernism, folklorism, etc., having crushed their literary careers and banned the publication of their works, having hounded them into alcoholism or suicide, or, more simply, having had them deported, that is to say, after having done what had had to be done, they had been inspired to come to the Gorky Institute to

complete their literary education. Some were members of
the Supreme Soviet of their respective republics and others
were prominent figures. One day, in an economics seminar
when we were discussing inflation, Shogentsukov had coolly
remarked, 'When I was prime minister I had to deal with
a similar problem.'

I was now walking along the dark part of the corridor.
I could see hardly anything, except the little bronze plaques
that I'm sure they all dreamed of having one day on their
shoddily gloss-painted doors: 'From 1958 to 1960 this room
was the home of the celebrated Abdullakhanov'; 'From 1955
to 1960 this room was the home of . . .' Wait! I almost
shouted. A pale beam of light could be seen at the base of
a nearby door. It was Anatoly Kuznetsov's. It must have
been his window I'd seen lit when I was in the taxi. So
Kuznetsov had got back from vacation before me. If anyone
had told me a minute before that somebody I knew was
inside this seven-storey Sahara I would have rushed to greet
him in a frenzy . . . One word, my brother, one word to
people this desert! But suddenly in my mind I could see
the eyes of the author of *Continuation of a Legend* – two
slits behind thick lenses – and I lowered the hand I'd raised
to knock at his door. I didn't like the man any more than
I liked Yuri Goncharov, whom one of the two Shotas said
was the most prominent writer of all the lands watered by
the Volga, while the other insisted that he was nothing more
than a police informer.

I began to walk slowly down the stairs. At one point
I thought I heard muffled voices and stopped to listen.
Perhaps Kuznetsov was reading aloud what he'd just been

writing. On the landing of the fifth floor I heard the sounds again. It was like a discreet invitation to stop. A resident had apparently gone into one of the rooms that looked onto the inner courtyard. I made my way through the murky half light of the corridor in the hope that he was someone I knew. Thanks to a glow coming from under a door, I soon discovered which room it was. It was indeed one of those that faced the courtyard but I didn't know who lived there. This floor was occupied by first-year students – we treated them with a degree of condescension. Despite that, I was about to knock on the door when I heard a voice coming from the room and suddenly remembered it belonged to a Chinese student, Ping, whom, for some unfathomable reason, we called Hundred Flower Bloom. He must have been reading aloud. I recalled his accent and his features and thought a screech-owl speaking Russian would have been easier to understand.

I moved away and carried on down the stairs. The other floors seemed to be dead. In the lobby Auntie Katya's beady eyes followed me without a trace of goodwill. As I went out I realised I had never needed human warmth more than I did that evening. Even if she were to revert to her former friendliness, to the particular variety of benevolence that most Russian babushkas exhibited towards foreign students, I would never forgive her the coldness she had shown me earlier.

When I got into the street, it had stopped raining. There weren't many people at the trolleybus stop. I felt a vibration in the overhead wires and then in the distance, as if emerging from a dream, I saw the stately stag coming towards me in the twilight, its antlers held high.

I got off at Pushkin Square. Gorky Street was brightly lit and as busy as ever. The block between the *Izvestia* newspaper building and the Moskva Hotel – the right-side pavement, especially – was the favoured promenade of the Gorky Institute crowd, perhaps because Herzen's old house, which had been turned into the Institute, was at the crossing of Tverskoy Boulevard and Moscow's main thoroughfare.

On the façade of the *Izvestia* building the neon board mentioned an exhibition of some kind and also the name of Richard Nixon. Ah! I thought. So there's an American exhibition in Sokolniki Park . . . . Other news, from Ukraine and the Urals, and of Khrushchev's departure on a trip abroad, or his return, was also streaming on the board but the moving letters made me dizzy and I turned away. At Central Cinema they were showing *Nights of Cabiria*, but I'd seen it in Riga. A crowd had assembled around the entrance.

Without thinking, I turned back to the *Izvestia* news board. On his arrival at the airport, Nikita Khrushchev had been met by the p r e s i d e n t of the Presidium. But L i d a S n e g i n a had not come to meet *me* at the Rizhsky Voksal. I felt depressed. On the pavement outside the cinema there was a newsstand and several phone booths. I wasn't angry with Lida, just sad. I went into one of the booths, inserted a coin, dialled the number and waited. The receiver smelt of tobacco. It occurred to me that perhaps this phone had been used to break off a relationship only a few moments earlier – I couldn't account for the oppressive, acrid stench in any other way. I was tempted to hang up but I didn't move, just waited. I forced myself to imagine Lida walking towards the telephone in high heels on a thick carpet (I've no idea why), her hair glinting gold and her stiff, straight neck keeping vulgarity at bay. Her hair and her neck, which always seemed to exude an electric fragrance, had struck me when I first saw her at a party with a Georgian man. Before I'd even glimpsed her face, I had learned her hair and neck. People are as recognisable by their necks as they are by their faces, yet in the days and weeks after our first encounter I was astounded by my own inability to memorise anything of her, save her neck. It was delicate and silky, and expressed its owner's coolness and warmth, in so far as reserve can be called coolness, and passion, warmth.

I don't know why but as I gazed at it, I felt that that fascinating, swan-like neck was threatened. It was perhaps a result of how my interest in that young woman first arose and perhaps because of all I had seen and heard in the corridors at my hall of residence, but that evening I imagined Lida Snegina's neck was threatened either by the teeth of loud-mouthed Abdullakhanov or those of the mumbling Kyuzengesh.

All around her reigned the usual hubbub of dancing parties at the Gorky Institute, whose special flavour arose from the contrast between the eternal glory of literature and its living embodiments either stumbling around the dance floor or talking nonsense. Those soirées were only really lively early in the evening when the girls were still entranced by the thought that they would soon meet an actual writer. Their suitors – Goethes, Villons and so forth – were all around them: celebrity was close, just look around. May I introduce my friend Piotr Reutsky? He's a poet. Have you read 'Dawn of the Birches'? He wrote it. Really? Yes, indeed, that's who he is . . . Over the chatter there hovered, as in a mist, the implication and the illusion that by meeting a writer you might become someone yourself and perhaps earn the right to have your initials at the head of a poem or a story, not to mention, later on, in posthumously published diaries, correspondence, memoirs, archives . . .

It was still the first half of the party (in the second, the truth would slowly emerge and the girls would begin to cast disdainful glances at their partners, to extricate themselves from their arms and occasionally, as happened to Nutfulla Shakenov, one would slap the face of a man with whom, only two hours earlier, she had dreamed of being entwined on a marble tombstone, her initials beside a line from the poem he would have dedicated to her, 'I remember our April, April in the icy Karakum . . .'). So, as I was saying, it was still the pink and jolly part of the evening, yet Lida Snegina was already regarding it with unaffected scorn. She seemed sorry to have come, while one of her girlfriends was beside herself with excitement. 'It's odd,' Lida explained to me later, once we had become better acquainted. 'She's an interesting person, but she has an irrational passion for writers. That one over there, he's a prose writer, isn't he?' She nodded towards a man called Kurganov. 'My friend waited four months for him to publish a story that was supposed to be about her. When the story appeared, it turned out to feature a milkmaid from the Lenin's Way collective farm! But my friend is quite happy because Kurganov managed to convince her that the milkmaid was a disguise for the true subject, which was her! I'm not sure what I would call that if it happened to me. How about you? Are you a writer as well?'

Aha, my little pigeon, I thought, you won't catch me out so easily! It took no great insight to guess that Lida did not like writers and that she had attached herself to me because I did not look like one. I shook my head and mumbled a few words to the effect that I did something in the cinema, regretting instantly that I hadn't invented a calling even more distant from literature, such as table-tennis or Egyptology. She asked if I was training as a scriptwriter, but to shield myself from danger I muttered that I was vaguely involved in translating subtitles but, to be honest, I didn't even do that . . . At the rate I was going I'd soon have downgraded myself to lighting assistant. At that point the band stopped playing and we parted.

Having asked her for the next dance, I told her I found it amazing that she had so little liking for writers when she was in their lair. She explained that she loved literature but mostly the works of dead authors. As for living writers, well, it was perhaps because she'd known two or three and maybe also because of her friend's experience, no, she didn't like them . . . I thought, It's the ballad of Doruntine and Kostandin all over again, with the quick and the dead on the same horse! I felt I wanted to tell her the old legend about the promise. But something, I don't know what, held me back.

Meanwhile her friend beamed as she danced beside us with Kurganov, and I whispered in Lida's ear that he was surely promising to put her in a novel and make her the deputy chair of the collective farm or a matronly militant heading a delegation from the Autonomous Republic of Belarus at an international peace conference.

Lida laughed, and I reckoned it was now or never that I should ask for her telephone number. The string of six glowing pearls emerged from her whole being, from the curve of her back, her legs, her groin and her breasts, her neck and her lips – half a dozen magical digits with which I could summon her voice from anywhere in the universe. I felt more exhausted than a pearl fisherman and finally, when she and her friend left, escorted by Kurganov, I said to myself, She really was one of the most interesting women I have ever met. I had one reservation: I feared she might be a little cool. However, when I called her a few days later and she answered in a warm, still sleepy voice that she had been waiting for me to ring, I decided my fears were unfounded. She was a medical student and we saw each other frequently throughout April, May and part of June, up to the start of the long vacation. Each time I rang it struck me as odd that some women have hidden inside them a peculiar device that turns their voices from the normal tone to the tone of love, rather like a transformer that turns electricity from 110 to 220 volts, or vice versa.

All of that was going through my mind as I stood in the telephone kiosk listening to the gaps between the ring tones and surrounded by the smell of stale tobacco. *Razluka*:

'Break-up'. Why hadn't anyone thought of that as a brand-name for cigarettes? It would surely be a winner. A packet of *Razluka*. Twenty *Rusalka*. A carton of *Rizhsky Voksal*.

I imagined her on her way to pick up the phone, holding herself so straight, and, in my mind, I mercilessly dismembered the Procrustean corridor of her lodgings, making it longer and longer to justify the time she was taking to get to the phone and pick up. At long last the fifteen kopecks dropped somewhere inside the call box – or, rather, into the pit of my stomach, like lead weights, as if they were coins from Herod's ancient kingdom. 'Hello?' said a quavery voice. It was her grandmother's. After a short period of muddle (What? Who? I see. Lida?), I was given to understand that she was away in the Crimea.

I left the phone booth, crossed Pushkin Square, and walked down Gorky Street, on the right-hand side, where young layabouts regularly hung around for hours on end, watching the girls go by. On the front of the *Izvestia* building, the news board went on streaming. Khrushchev was going on another trip. For some time now papers had been calling him Nikitushka or Nikitinka, affectionate diminutives used for folk heroes like Ilya Muromets and so forth. Every time I'd tried to call Lida 'Lidushka' or 'Lidochka' she had burst out laughing because I put the stress on the wrong syllable, the last, as if I was speaking Albanian. So, Lida was now at the midpoint of her summer, as I had been at the middle of mine a few days previously, in Dubulti. As I walked on I was overcome with the desire to talk about the weather, about the summer, about anything at all to anyone I could find, even a statue. In front of me stood the huge central post office building. Brigita, the Latvian girl I'd met! Why hadn't I thought of calling her sooner? I almost ran up the steps to the post office. Brigita had left Dubulti two days before I had. She must be home now in Riga, in one of those comfortable old apartments with a big ceramic stove taking up almost a whole wall and heavy oak furniture. I liked that town – where it would soon be getting cold – with its grey buildings, the turrets that resembled knights' helmets, its ancient cobbled streets, their names mostly ending with -*baum*.

I gave the number to an operator and sat on a bench waiting for the call to be put through. Drawling voices announced names of faraway places that I thought had disappeared long ago. Magadan, Astrakhan, and even more legendary cities (apparently, you could call up the whole Golden Horde!), and I felt as if something was being extinguished inside me. I thought it must be from here that Kyuzengesh phoned his desolate tundra late in the afternoon, smoothing it with the low rustle of his voice, promising it who knew what in the twilight hours when sparse flocks of birds flew low overhead in the gloomy not-night and not-day that lasted six full months of the year.

I imagined that Brigita was perhaps still indoors, that she hadn't gone for a walk in the -*baum* streets. In the last week of my holiday in Riga the weather had been bad and rain had often forced us to take refuge in cinemas where they were showing films we had already seen, in cafés we'd just left or even in some Protestant church where a service was being held. We'd been several times to Dzintari and to all the other stations with names that reminded me of beauty products, and now the smell of her hair had got mixed up with the smell of her toothpaste and her lips, which she made up only a little, to save them from getting chapped by the sea wind, into a single scent that belonged to all those railway stops.

The operator called my name. I went into a booth and said, 'Hello! Hello!' several times. At the other end someone said something in Latvian that, of course, I didn't understand, while in the next booth a coarse voice was speaking with Samarkand or maybe the Karakum – I recognised the simple sounds of an Eastern tongue. Another voice broke in on my line, in an unknown language, then a burst of interference, and I thought I heard Latvian again, then yet more distant and plaintive voices. Almost losing hope in this transcontinental cackle, I blurted out her name, which was immediately swallowed, shredded, crumbled and ingested by the sand and peat of the marshes, by the taiga and the Northern Lights, leaving on the surface nothing more than a bleak hunger for more names, maybe for my own, with an accompaniment of pitiful sighs. I hung up and stumbled out of the post office. As I cut through the passing crowds I was suddenly afflicted with an unbearable headache that beat against my skull, boom! boom! as if the streets of Riga were thrashing me with the rubber mallets of their -baum, -baum endings.

On Okhotny Ryad the dun-coloured rain-drenched crowd milled between the huge Gosplan building and the Moskva Hotel. You could just about see the outline of the Bolshoi in the distance and, further behind it, in a welter of mauve and blue lights, the older building of the Metropole, the hotel where only foreigners stayed, and where you would also occasionally see a police van carting away prostitutes. I slowed, dithering between a right turn along Kuznetsky Most, a left turn into the narrow and noisy Peredelkinorovka Street, or even going on up to Red Square. Any solitary walker would have taken the first option, but curiously, without knowing why, I went on towards the square that everyone who has never lived in Moscow believes to be the heart of the city. In fact anyone walking in the evening towards Red Square can feel the floods of people in Gorky Street run dry as they approach its shore – the crowds thin out and only a few people push on as far as the ancient esplanade, like the thinning blood of an anaemic trying to make its way to the brain. If the GUM department store facing the Kremlin weren't there to draw people in, Red Square would surely be one of the most desolate quarters of Moscow.

GUM must still have been open because people were milling about on the pavement in front of it. On the other side of the square, outside the Historical Museum, there wasn't a soul. I carried on at a leisurely pace and came onto Red Square. Although I passed along Gorky Street pretty much every day and almost as often crossed Sverdlov Square, the Arbat and Tverskoy Boulevard, as well as Dzerzhinsky Square, where the number three trolleybus left for Butyrki, I hardly ever found my way to Red Square, and only on Sundays. Perhaps my disinclination derived from the disappointment I had felt on first seeing the Kremlin's rust-coloured bastions. There was something unfinished, apathetic and undramatic about those squat brick walls, with their haughty towers poking up here and there. Perhaps

I felt like that because I had grown up in a town overlooked by a citadel that was tens of metres high, with towers that were sometimes above the clouds and ramparts from which, even now, a thousand years after they were built, large blocks of stone sometimes came loose and fell to earth, like bolts of lightning, crushing houses and killing people in their path. By contrast, the somnolent, placid walls of the Kremlin gave off a ruddy cheerfulness that sterilised the imagination. No dashing horseman with moonlight glinting on his steel visor would bring any message to the gates of this castle; through its doors had come only ponderous, leather-robed monks from the Novodevichy Monastery, chanting Church Slavonic and surrounded by the false Dmitrys who had woven the fabric of Russian history.

Some of these thoughts whirled in my mind as I walked along the side of the ancient fortress. In the blue-tinted light of the evening the cupolas of St Basil's looked like the turbans of our own Bektashi preachers or like coloured soap bubbles blown by some gigantic mouth. Slavic myths tell of a terrifying head all alone in the middle of the steppe that puffs out its cheeks to blow the great wind that raises the dust-storm. That wind is so strong that no rider who dares to come before it – even if he keeps as far away as the horizon – can stay on his horse. Every time I read anything about that head I tingled with fright, despite the absence of bloodshed and mystery. But perhaps that was exactly what made me shiver: a fall caused by wind and earth in a vast empty flatness with only that head rising from it. 'It would be better not to have myths like that!' Maskiavicius sometimes remarked. 'It really does belong to steppe and dust. Stunted Slavic divinities . . . But you Balkan folk have legends of a different class — they're almost as good as Lithuanian folklore! But what's the use? Socialist realism forbids us to write about them.' That was what Maskiavicius used to say, but you couldn't rely on him. He changed his opinions as often as his shirts.

I crossed the square and walked along the pavement outside GUM, as far as the monument to Minin and Pozharsky, raised on a plinth originally used as an executioner's block. From that corner the Kremlin walls looked even more peaceful. A muddled voice in my head told me that castles weren't more or less Macbethical or Buddhistical solely by virtue of the grey or red colouring of their walls or their more or less mysterious shapes, but from the fretwork-like appearance of their turrets. The same voice also told me that, behind its casual ruddy face, this half-European and half-Asiatic castle soon would, or maybe already did, contain a great mystery. The block where heads had been severed was still there, not far from the walls, like a moon hovering over the horizon.

I suddenly remembered the police summons that Auntie Katya had handed me, then almost told myself aloud that I was exhausted and ought to get back to the hall of residence.

It was still just as empty and dark as it had been when I had gone out, and I wondered where I could go to kill time that night, even for an hour: to Anatoly Kuznetsov's or Chinese Ping's? I didn't really want to be with either of them and felt I would prefer to be alone in my room.

I began climbing towards the sixth floor. I recalled the monastic silence of the corridors in the Writers' Residence in Yalta, with Ladonshchikov's furtive footfalls on the carpeted floor, and Valentin, Paustovsky's driver, who told us one day, between two hiccups, his eyes glazed from drink, that he was being tormented by the writer's wife, a harridan who was wrecking his life, and that if he was still driving that car it was out of loyalty to Konstantin Paustovsky: if it hadn't been for him he wouldn't have stayed a minute longer in the job – he'd rather drive a pig lorry, a manure truck or a hearse than set eyes on that woman's snout again. But there was nothing Konstantin could do about it, he went on, when he had calmed down. She had been a present to Paustovsky from that carrot-haired pig called Arbuzov – that guy who wrote plays with which he, Valentin, wouldn't deign to wipe his arse, seeing as Arbuzov could never rise above Konstantin Georgevich, and had failed to bring down Paustovsky with insults and had not managed to poison him or have him deported or infect him with a contagious disease. The worst Arbuzov could do to Paustovsky was to palm off his own ghastly wife on him. When he got to that point in his tale Valentin usually looked round to see if there was still any benighted soul who did not know that Paustovsky's current wife had previously been married to Arbuzov. He had landed him with the woman, Valentin would go on, once he had made certain everyone was in the know, and ruined his life, because otherwise Konstantin Georgevich, not that fuckwit Fedin, would be president of the Writers' Union, and Valentin would be driving not Paustovsky's blue Volga saloon but a luxury Zim limousine and would be getting three hundred roubles a month more in wages.

I don't know why I kept going over Valentin's monologues. I tried to turn my mind to other things but curiously it kept coming back to Valentin. Was it because I had previously heard those soliloquies in other empty corridors on nights that were just as boring and far away from everybody else? I should have got out of the corridor if I wanted to silence the whispering inside me. Run away, yes – but where to? I no longer felt like shutting myself away in my room. I had Lida's voice on one of my tapes. She lay there as if she were in a long, magical coffin, without body or hair, just her voice. No! Keep me away from that tape recorder. And suddenly, as my whole being sought a place to escape and forget, I remembered the left wing of the huge building. It was almost always empty and served as a reservoir of rooms that might be allocated to teachers from the Gorky Institute, or to house guests of the Writers' Union, or as temporary digs for writers who had walked out on their wives and didn't know where else to go. Some evenings when I'd had a bit to drink I used to enjoy visiting that deserted wing. I had a key to one of the empty apartments. In a way it was my second home, a second silent, secret abode. 'Want to come to my *dacha*?' I once asked Lida Snegina, during a lively party, and dragged her by the hand into the dark corridors of the left wing. She was fascinated by that uninhabited suite on whose walls and ceilings the distant headlights of cars left translucent streaks, like those of garden snails.

Let loneliness cure loneliness, I thought, as I went

through my pockets looking for the key. Once I had found it I trekked over to the left wing. The floorboards creaked softly beneath my feet. I found the door, opened it and went inside. I fumbled along the wall for the light switch. The walls hadn't changed, the floral paper with its green background reminding me of funerals. I went into one of the rooms and stood there for a minute, my hands in my pockets, as if I had frozen. I went to the door to the other room in the suite, but as soon as I had turned on the light, I really did freeze: someone had sullied my sanctuary. I was dumbfounded. My eyes lighted on a corner of the room where there lay an empty bottle, a tin of food, and an object I could not make out. I stepped two paces forward and noticed that next to the bottle there was a torn piece of wrapping paper that must have been used for something greasy. Further on lay a few sheets of paper. I bent down. It was typescript, with closely spaced lines. Nothing else. It looked as if the intruder had come here to drink vodka and read the pages, which perhaps he hadn't liked because he had left them behind with the remnants of his meal. For a second I thought he was going to come back, jerk open the door and take me by surprise. But the leftovers in the tin had dried out. I knelt down to gather up the typed sheets. There must have been two or three hundred. At first glance the characteristic lay-out of Russian dialogue told me I was holding a literary work. The beginning – possibly the first half (with the title page, obviously) – was missing. The page numbering went from 304 to 514. I was about to put the script back on the floor, but my eyes automatically

began to run across the top sheet, which was the opening
of a Chapter 31:

'Zhivago, Zhivago,' Strelnikov went on repeating to
himself in his coach, to which they had just passed.
'From merchants. Or the nobility. Well, yes: a doctor
from Moscow . . .'

I jumped forty or forty-five pages and landed on this
sentence:

He analyses and interprets Dostoevsky's *Possessed* and
The Communist Manifesto with equal enthusiasm, and
it seems to me . . .

I would have read on, but a handful of pages slipped from
my grasp, and as I bent down to gather them, I lost my
place in the typescript. I hurriedly leafed through the rest
of the work and only stopped on the very last sheet to
read the line where the text broke off:

Outside it was snowing. Wind shovelled the snow
everywhere. It was falling more and more thickly, more
densely, as if in pursuit of something, and Yuri
Andreyevich looked out of the window at it as if it
wasn't snow but . . .

What is this? I wondered. I had thought at first it might
have been left behind by whoever had been drinking in
the room, but as I recalled the phrase about Dostoyevsky

and *The Communist Manifesto* it struck me it might be a forbidden work circulating from hand to hand. Such things had become quite common in recent times. Three months before, late one night, or maybe just before dawn, Maskiavıcıus had knocked on my door – or, rather, collapsed in front of it in a state of complete inebriation – and when I opened it he had shoved a handful of type-script sheets towards me and slurred, 'Take this and read what he said, this guy, that's right, it's Dante Tvardovsky, oops, I mean Marguerite, sorry, I meant to say Aleksandr Alighieri . . .' It had taken me all of fifteen minutes to work out that the pages contained a banned poem by Aleksandr Tvardovsky called 'Vasily Tyorkin in the Other World'.

I left the pile of papers where I'd found them, next to the vodka bottle, the tin and the wrapping paper. Then, having cast a last glance over the depressing still-life, I switched off the light and went out.

The only place left for me to go now was my room. I was worn out and lay down on my bed, but although I tried hard, I managed to reach only the outer rim of the Valley of Sleep, the colourless, soundless foothills far removed from the picturesque heartland of my dreams. I could hear the crackling of the current in the overhead wires when trolleybuses pulled into the stop. Those fairytale stags wanted to take me to the centre of town but they were quite lost as they swam about in the sky, their antlers pronging the clouds, while beneath their bellies lay nameless winding grey streets waiting for us to crash into them.

★

Three days later the graduates and teaching staff of the Gorky Institute's two degree courses started coming back. The great house awoke. The first from our class to arrive was Ladonshchikov, his stagy smile expressing his satisfaction with himself and with the fine running order of the great Soviet Union. His cheeks bore a permanent blush, as if they were lit by some kind of fever, suggesting both the high pomp of a plenary session and emotion spilling over from meetings with his readers and superannuated heroines of Soviet Labour, and an eager Party spirit holding his bureaucratic eminence in check. Similarly, his putty-coloured raincoat, tailored to look almost like a uniform, was cheerful and modest at the same time. If you looked at him closely, especially when he was saying, 'So that's how it is, comrades' – *Vot tak, tovarishchi* – you might well think that his face had provided the model for all the directives from the leadership of the Union of Soviet Writers about matters concerning the positive hero and maybe even for a number of the decisions that had been taken on the issue. Ladonshchikov's face brought all those tedious questions to mind. He let his Soviet smile fall in only one circumstance: when the topic was Jews. He would turn into another man: his movements would go out of synch, the relative quantities of optimism and pessimism expressed on his face would be inverted, and phrases like *Vot tak, tovarishchi* made way for different and often vulgar ones. But all the same, on those rare occasions, even though what he said was repulsive, he seemed more human, because the stench of manure and pig shit he gave off was at least real. I'd seen him in that state several times last winter in Yalta when he was spying at Paustovsky's window. But at times like that one of the Shotas used to say, 'No, don't be scared of Ladonshchikov!' In his view it was when he was in that sort of a state that Ladonshchikov became harmless. It was the pink, pompous smiling state that made him dangerous: that was when he could have you sent to Butyrky Prison with a click of his fingers, as he had done a year ago to two of his colleagues. Shota's words returned to me every time I came out of the metro station at Novoslobodskaya Street and walked past the endless reddish walls of the prison.

The two Shotas came back together that day. Over the holidays they had squabbled many times in cafés in Tbilisi and cursed each other roundly; then, most bizarrely, they had ended up in the same writers' retreat, had argued and thrown insults at each other, one accusing the other of being glued to his heels, and vice versa, then had decided to give up on holidays and leave for who knew where; although there were hosts of trains every day from Georgia to Moscow, they had ended up travelling not only on the same service but in the same carriage!

The next day Hieronymus Stulpanc and Maskiavicius, our fellow students from the Baltic, turned up, both tipsy; next came the 'Belarusian Virgins' (that's what we called the girls on our course, though only one was from Belarus). The Karakums, as we referred to those from Central Asia, all turned up around midnight, blind drunk, with Taburokov in tow. He'd been flailing about, trying to force his way into the Israeli Embassy because he wanted to have a word – just a word – with the Jewish ambassador to salve his conscience. So the bastard would not be able to claim afterwards that Taburokov hadn't warned him in time, as his writer's conscience required him to, and that he'd already changed alphabet three times, yes, he had, and all that that came with, and he didn't really care anyway, and as a matter of fact he'd be happy to piss in the Jordan, however sacred it was. And that wouldn't do us any harm either, because we've strangled all the Volgas and Olgas in their cradles, along with their alphabets, because we had Cyril and Methodius and the glorious Soviet sandpit and the one and indivisible— Brrr! It's freezing in here!

Artashez Pogosian, nicknamed 'The Masses in Their Tens of Millions' because he identified with them all at the drop of a hat, apparently delighted to have dumped his wife, swept in with the other students from the Caucasus. They were all drunk, except Shogentsukov, who had come on his own on a later train, and turned up looking slightly drained, his face exhibiting what Pogosian jokingly called his post-prime-ministerial melancholy.

That same day saw the Moldovans come in, as well as the Russians from Siberia and Central Russia, including Yuri Goncharov (nicknamed 'Yuri Donoschik' by one of the Shotas, who thought he was a government sneak); then came the Jews, the Tatars and the Ukrainians, the only ones who came by plane. The next day Kyuzengesh arrived in the afternoon, looking quite grey, the last of the group. As was his habit, he shut himself away in his room and did not emerge for forty-eight hours. Stulpanc, who occupied the room next door, said that he always did that when he came back from the tundra because he found it hard to readjust to twenty-four-hour days. It was a serious problem for writers from those parts, Stulpanc went on. Can you imagine living your whole life in six-month-long days and nights, and then being required to divide your time into artificial chunks when you sit down to write? For instance, Kyuzengesh couldn't write 'Next morning he left' because 'next morning' for him meant in six months' time. Or again, when a writer from the tundra set down 'Night fell', he was recording something that happened so rarely it would have the same effect as 'The third Five-year Plan has been launched' or 'War has broken out'. 'Our comrades from the tundra have a problem,' Stulpanc went on. 'One night Kyuzengesh said something to me but he spoke so softly I couldn't understand anything. But he was definitely complaining about all that. I reckon someone ought to look in detail at the *time* factor in the writing of our friends from the tundra. It's got real potential, even if it comes close to the kind of modernism people say that French fellow Proust fell into when he made time go round in circles. Socialist realism needs to be studied in its impact on the Arctic plains, don't you agree?'

'Stulpanc, you really don't know what you're saying,' Nutfulla Shakenov broke in. 'You're trying to tell me about that decadent Procrustes, or whatever his name is, but do you realise that in all the tundra and the taiga put together, in an area of three million square kilometres and then some, there is one, and only one, writer and that's Kyuzengesh? Do we really need a literary theory just for him?'

We all thought that was ominous and grandiose at the same time. To be lord and master in a space more than six times the size of Europe! To be the tundra's own grey consciousness!

There were crowds of people in the corridors of Herzen's old two-storey house and outside it, in the garden with the iron railings and two gates, the main one on Tverskoy Boulevard and the other at the rear giving on to Malaya Bronnaya. Nowhere else in the world could so many dreams of eternal glory be crowded into such a small space. Often, when you looked at all those ordinary faces in profile – some fresh and alert, most of them drawn and unkempt – you might guess that several were already turning into marble or bronze. That became obvious when, around dusk and especially when they were drunk, a one-armed fourth-year student and Nutfulla Shakenov, with his partly destroyed nose, resembled statues dug clumsily out of the ground by an archaeologist.

The corridors were crammed mostly with first-year students. They appeared drunk, and had a euphoric glow, as if they had been pumped full of gamma rays, while their pallor was graced with a layer of perspiration that was as becoming as it was permanent. A boy with sparkling, close-set eyes wove among them – a slim, handsome lad who had come from the Altai mountains. He moved from one group to another, getting into conversation with some, saying whatever flashed into his mind, then taking off to talk to another knot of people. 'What a splendid pair of trousers!' he exclaimed to me. 'Where did you get them?' His wide eyes became even more entrancing. 'Where did you find them?' I told him, curtly, because I was rather cross that he should use familiar forms of language with me when I was his senior. He noticed my irritation, bowed two or three times, his hand on his chest in apology, and said he would henceforth adopt a more formal tone, would speak to me in the third or fourth person, if it existed, but that I should not take offence: he came from the highlands of the Altai where men were more frank and open than they were anywhere else. 'You, you,' he kept saying with a smile, because it was the only word of English he knew, and I told him he'd pronounced it as if it was an Albanian word. That was when he twigged I was from Albania, and declared passionately that he would wear only Albanian trousers in future because they were the most stylish in the world. Then he asked if I could give him the pattern, and blurted out that he wanted everything he had to be perfect, that he would write perfect works, that within the next month he would meet the prettiest girl in Moscow and have an affair with her. 'I am a virgin,' he went on, in breathless excitement, 'and, like the Altai mountains with their sublime peaks, I insist on losing my virginity to the most inaccessible girl in the capital!' He carried on talking with unaltered fervour, but instead of blushing he grew even paler. 'That is how it is! I have to manage this at any cost, because if I don't, I don't know what I will do. How lucky I am to make your acquaintance. Oh! Sorry, to make your acquaintance, *sir*. I'll begin with the trousers. A man who hasn't got the right kind of trousers doesn't deserve any favours from life. I only like things that are perfect because I'm from the Altai and up there everything is noble, pure and eternal. I can't have a fling with an ordinary girl. She'll be either the most beautiful or there'll be nobody . . .'

'Well,' I replied, entertained, 'it'll be very hard to get everything, so to speak, up to the same height as the Altai.'

He broke in energetically, 'No, sir, you'll never persuade me of that. You've got the best trousers in Moscow, so please tell me where I can find the most attractive girl in town!'

I smiled and was about to tell him that he would never find what he was after, even with the help of the KGB, but his eyes latched on to mine, like a cat's, and he seemed to expect that I was about to tell him the name and address of Sleeping Beauty and maybe her telephone number too.

CHAPTER THREE

To my left, beyond the window's double panes, snow was falling noiselessly; to my right, in complete contrast, the dark smudge of Nutfulla Shakenov's rough, tanned chin, was bent low over his notes. Wet snow slithered intermittently over Tverskoy Boulevard, settling on the trees and empty benches. The letters that Nutfulla Shakenov was writing in his notebook were widely spaced, as if he were bewildered. The professor of aesthetics was lecturing on the eternal unity of life and art. Sometimes the snow seemed to settle on his sentences, giving them a melancholic and meandering cast. He was explaining that art goes hand in hand with life from the moment of birth, when the infant is greeted with song, until death, when funeral music accompanies a man's last journey to the grave. Drowsy with the heat rising from the radiators, I gazed at the passers-by as they hurried, wrapped up in themselves, along Tverskoy Boulevard and speculated that sometimes art is bound up with the icy snow sweeping people on to Gorky Street, the Garden Ring or the Arbat. It made them put their heads down, hunch their shoulders, and pick tiny grains of ice from their eyelids. 'Art does not abandon us even after death,' the lecturer droned on. Even after death, I parroted in my mind. Snow falls on us all even after death, that's for sure . . . Nutfulla, beside me, carried on writing his misshapen black letters. In the row in front of mine Antaeus, from Greece, was muttering something to Hieronymus Stulpanc. The two Shotas, sitting beside him, looked horrified. 'And so, for example,' the lecturer was saying, 'some people's tombs are decorated with sculpture, or simply with an epitaph, a few lines of verse. Art accompanies them even in everlasting sleep . . .' He paused, presumably to measure the effect his words had had, which he must have judged insufficient, since he went on: 'A month ago I went to the Novodevichy monastery. I visit the cemetery there quite often. It was very autumnal. I stopped at the tomb of A. P. Kern, on which Pushkin's famous lines are carved:

'Я помню чудное мгновенье
Передо мной явилась ты . . .
I remember that magical moment
When you appeared before me . . .'

'Who was A. P. Corn?' Taburokov asked.

Taken aback, the lecturer turned to face him. His grey hair looked electric with anger. He opened his mouth several times before he could find his words. As if something was missing.

'You ought to know the answer, Taburokov,' he said at last. 'Every schoolboy knows that poem by heart. It's one of the most beautiful poems in all the world, and everyone knows that it is dedicated to a young lady with whom Pushkin had had an affair.'

'Oh, I see,' Taburokov said.

'Yes, you do, and don't forget it.'

'Pff!' Taburokov scowled. 'I can't remember the name of my first wife yet I'm supposed to remember someone called Anna Corn or Kerr or some such nonsense!'

'Don't say such things!' the lecturer screeched, anger making his voice rasp.

The audience, lulled into torpor by the whiteness of the snow outdoors, the warmth of the radiators inside and a general lack of interest in aesthetics, now woke up. Taburokov – he was bald, had a round, fleshy face and bags under his eyes – kept quiet. Stulpanc used to say that he looked like the bad guy in Chinese movies. He had a point. Taburokov's ashen scalp, with its greenish tinge, which was visible especially at twilight, looked like a guglet brought out of an archaeological dig, as if at night Taburokov fell not into sleep but into a hole in the ground.

It took several minutes for everyone to quieten down again. The lecturer, despite his irritation, returned to the cemetery of the Novodevichy monastery. I'd been there the previous year and his description was accurate, except that I could no longer recall if the russet leaves on the marble tombs were copper inlays or actual autumn leaves. Among the tombstones I'd noticed that of Stalin's wife, which had these words carved on it: 'To my beloved Alliluyeva, J. Stalin'.

As the lecturer carried on, silence settled over the room, perhaps because the topic was tombs and everyone was surely thinking about their own or about their verse being carved on the graves of women they had known, who perhaps didn't deserve the honour, because in most cases the affairs had consisted principally of disappointments and dubious consequences.

The group had now returned to its slumber. But it was of an unusual kind: it had a crack across it and a great howl ran the whole length of the scar. Snow was falling near to me, but it allowed me only brief escapes from the inner scream that was tearing everything to pieces. Nutfulla Shakenov's glance – olive-tinted, cloudy and blank at the core – almost touched my right eye. Indeed, his impressive eyebrow came within a whisker of sticking to my forehead, like a leech. Someone nearby sighed. 'Oh!' Was it Shogentsukov? No, not him. His face expressed some muffled sorrow. Next to him was Hieronymus Stulpanc, his yellow hair as translucent as a watercolour. Out of the corner of my eye I observed Shogentsukov's gelatinous visage and thought that it was perhaps not disappointment at losing his job (his ex-prime-ministerial pain, *dixit* Pogosian) that had wrought havoc on his huge head. The wailing that whirled around inside him, hollowing him out, like a drill, must have had some other root. In fact, everybody's nerves were somewhat on edge, but no gestures expressed an anxiety whose muteness made it all the more fearsome. It had been floating over us for some days. I'd noticed the first symptoms the previous Friday, when Abdullakhanov had said, 'Brothers, something's not right! *Shto-to nye to!*' For the rest of the afternoon and evening, people had stalked the corridors, bumping into things and cursing doors they seemed not to have noticed.

As for Taburokov . . . I suddenly realised why his question about A. P. Kern had been so incongruous. It was the second time he'd asked something like that. The first was just before the big party at which Maskiavicius had injured himself by walking into the glass panel of the main door, and the two Shotas went up to the attic of the Institute, over the ceiling of the seventh floor, to slug it out undisturbed. Just before this monumental drinking session, which was reported all the way up to the Executive Committee of the Writers' Union of the USSR, Taburokov, in a class on the psychology of artistic creation, had suddenly asked who Boris Godunov was, because he'd never heard of him before.

The question he asked today was just as bizarre. The first symptoms had appeared on Thursday or earlier, maybe as far back as Tuesday. Gloom had hung over us, a sense of the foreboding and depression that are so well expressed by the heavy sound of the Russian word *khandra* . . .

At last the lecture ended. Everyone went into the corridor and put on hats and coats, but nobody ventured outside. People were hovering, as if they were caught in fog, not knowing where the door was, and were watching each other for a signal or a message. At long last the signal came. As sharp as a razor blade and as supple as sunshine finding its way through the clouds, the gleaming word 'ski' was heard. It was a password, a code shared by all. Tomorrow, Sunday, skiing at Peredelkino. Of course, skiing, s k i i ng. A mad glint lit everyone's eyes. Abdullakhanov's close-set squinters. Maskavicius's too. The Shotas' four eyes casting their converging glances. The omnipresent photographic eyes of Yuri Goncharov. Even Taburokov and the Karakums uttered the word 'ski'. Aha! Now I guessed what the code was. The plot was unmasked. They said 'ski', but they heard 'vodka'! Well, then, tomorrow, at Peredelkino . . . The conspirators carried on exchanging glances. Kyuzengesh's eyes were veiled by what looked like a thin layer of ice (the frost had set in some time ago in the tundra). The eyes of Antaeus the Greek. Who then proposed, 'How about a coffee at the Praga?'

The Praga cafe on the Arbat was the only place in Moscow where you could get proper black coffee. They served it in little brass thimbles, and almost everyone in artistic and literary circles was a regular there. But Antaeus and I went to the Praga to satisfy our yearning for Balkan coffee.

We set off along Tverskoy Boulevard. The mix of rain and snow was oppressive.

'Seems like tomorrow is set to be a real binge!'

'So it seems.'

Antaeus and I used to spend a lot of time together. After the defeat of the Greek partisans at the Battle of Grammos,[*] he'd crossed the border into Albania with some of his comrades and for a time was given medical care in Gjirokastër, my home town. I was then in middle school, and I remember that when I spent nights in the area near the municipal hospital, I used to quake with fear when I heard the moanings of the wounded Greeks. 'I might even

[*] After the end of the Second World War, Communist partisans engaged in armed struggle for the control of Greece. They were finally defeated in September 1949 at a battle in the Grammos region.

have heard your groans,' I used to tell Antaeus. He'd been living in Moscow for a while now and spent his time writing; since he'd been sentenced to death *in absentia* in Greece he had no intention of setting foot in his own land ever again.

'Tomorrow there'll be quite a shindig,' he said, once we were sitting in the café. 'You remember the last time?'

I nodded, signalling something like, Yes, sure, there'll be chaos. 'It's all because of boredom,' I said. 'A kind of collective *khandra*, don't you reckon?'

'It's affected us as well. We've got *khandra* too,' he replied. 'Isn't that so?'

I didn't know what to say. Though I had broached the subject I wasn't keen on his going over it again. I trusted him, we'd told each other a lot of things held to be sensitive and yet, I don't know why, I'd recently become much less open with him on matters of this kind.

'Antaeus,' I said, 'we've known each other for ages, yet I've never thought of asking you what your real name is.'

He smiled, turned to gaze through the window at the crowd thronging the steps to the Arbat Metro station, then, without looking at me directly and speaking in a muted voice, as if he was referring to something very far away, he uttered his name. Then he turned to me and asked, 'You don't like it, do you?'

I shrugged in a gesture that meant approximately, 'That's not the point, but . . .' To be honest, compared to his *nom de guerre*, Antaeus, his real name struck me as very plain. It was a perfectly ordinary Greek name with a *th* sound and several *ss* in it.

'I can understand your not liking it,' he said, as he took off his glasses to wipe the lenses. Like those of any short-sighted person without their glasses, his eyes looked wishy-washy and pale, like his name. 'You're not the first person to react in that way to my name. But my pseudonym is a different kettle of fish.'

The waiter brought us the brass thimbles and poured our coffee into them.

'To tell the truth, I've grown unaccustomed to my own name. I've spent most of my life under one alias or another.'

'Have you had many?'

He nodded. 'Yes, a few . . . I had to change them frequently, especially when I was underground.'

'And Antaeus is the latest?'

He shook his head melancholically. 'I think it's the last.' Staring through the window at the station entrance, Antaeus recited his various *noms de guerre* in a low voice. Almost all were names from classical tragedies, and for a second I saw him covered with tough, sword-proof scales that had come from ancient times to protect his soft, mortal flesh. Perhaps he felt that such anachronistic armour made him safe; perhaps, too, he could hear circling tambourines playing seductive rhythms, aiming to draw him on so he would stick out his head and be struck down . . . I'd seen how hedgehogs can be deceived by music when they roll up into a ball.

'The last,' he repeated, 'and the unluckiest.'

I knew what he meant: 'Antaeus' was the alias he'd been using at the time of the defeat, in 1949.

'You don't know what it's like when a comrade in arms

spits on you and you have no right to avenge that spit of shame,' he said. 'Antaeus is the name I was using when that happened to me. Did I tell you about it?'

'No.'

'"Antaeus, raise your head, raise your head, for God's sake . . ." I can still hear the words.' He brought the thimble to his lips and turned it upside down as if he wanted to empty it, except that there wasn't a drop of coffee left in it. A trace of the dregs stuck to the edge of his mouth. 'It happened to me the day after we had crossed the border . . . The Albanian border,' he added, after a pause.

'I recall the first lorries that brought Greek partisans into Gjirokastër.' I'd interrupted him, in an intentionally casual tone, hoping to lessen the level of drama that always loomed when conversation turned to the defeat of the Greek insurrection.

'It's imprinted on my mind,' he continued, without hearing what I'd said. 'We were in a mountain gorge, there was constant drizzle, and your soldiers' helmets were gleaming. We were harassed, muddy and bloodied − most of us were wounded; some were delirious, and as if that weren't enough, there he was, a terrifying figure, propped up on his crutches, hurling insults at us. Boy, did he give us hell! "Antaeus, raise your head, you faker!"'

'Who was that?' I enquired calmly. 'Who was insulting you?'

'Hang on, didn't I ever tell you his name?'

'No, you didn't.'

'He was a comrade in arms, an old militant who'd been wounded more than once and been put right abroad, on your side, in fact, at Gjirokastër. On his last stay in hospital he'd had both legs amputated, and though he was an invalid and only half alive he'd come to wait for us at the border, beneath a cliff, a few metres from the place where, after crossing into Albanian territory, we surrendered our weapons. He swore at us because we'd been beaten. Boy, did he insult us! He called us cowards, deserters, namby-pambies, fools. His hair, face and clothes were soaking but his tears were mixed with the rain. Only his voice gave away that he was sobbing. We were marching with our heads down and his harsh words struck sidelong blows on our wounds. Strangely, nobody answered him back. Our fighters marched on without turning their heads to either side. He recognised me: "Antaeus, raise your head!" he yelled, anger, tears and hurt breaking his voice. Like everyone else, I cast down my weapons and carried on. I could see nothing but I heard him shouting again, "Antaeus, raise your head, you fraud!" From the side he was waving a rake or some other imple-ment that seemed to be directed at my eyes. In the end I did raise my head, and that was when he spat on me. I walked on, moving further away from him as he carried on bawling and jigging about on his crutches, like he was being crucified, in the rain, a rain I'll never forget . . .' For the third time Antaeus sipped at his empty cup. 'So that's how it was!' he said, with a tap of his finger on the table top.

'Yes, those were grandiose and terrible events.'

'And now I give lectures, go to conferences, write theory . . .'

'Things have calmed down more or less everywhere,' I said, with a smile. 'Have you noticed our embarrassment when we hear people talk about the epic spirit of the old revolutionary struggle? We're like schoolboys when their parents come up from the provinces to visit them, wearing old-fashioned greatcoats.'

'I see what you mean.'

'It's like the alias business,' I went on. 'If you ever took on another clandestine job, I don't think you'd look to the tragedies for a new pseudonym—'

Smiling, he interrupted: 'Do you mean I'd take one from a comedy? Go on being ironic! I've got a thick skin, I can take it. When all's said and done, I'm a defeated man.'

In the few words he'd just spoken, I saw a suggestion of vulnerability, and shouted, 'It's impossible to have a conversation with you any more! You're always so prickly!'

In fact this was the first time he had seemed to take offence, and we had never quarrelled before.

'That's true,' he said. 'I'm on edge, over-sensitive. Anyway, take no notice. Please, go on. What were you saying about pseudonyms?'

'Let's talk about something else.'

He laughed. 'I can guess what you're thinking,' he said. 'You see an ex-militant who's now a peaceable Muscovite. With a fur collar on his coat and a pair of bedroom slippers, Antaeus has become the very model of the petit-bourgeois. What a character! Am I right?'

'Typical characters arise in typical situations. Isn't that what Engels said?' I joked.

'True, in typical circumstances . . . In typical circumstances,' he said again, nodding. 'Yes, of course, with baby fox fur and slippers as soft as the southern breeze on his bedside rug . . .' He looked around for his coffee cup, but the waiter had already cleared it away.

'So my aliases are just stage names!' he said, as if to himself. 'Be honest: isn't that what you think of me?'

I'd actually said that as a general observation, not directly about him. I'd never thought about the matter at any length. It was just that in the atmosphere of the lives we led, ancient and legendary names, like Prometheus, Antaeus and so on, didn't sit well with the activists I'd encountered at the Soviet Writers' Retreat. At most they might use aliases from opera or, if it had to be a classical reference, then perhaps Dionysus . . .

I laid that out quite bluntly while insisting that my observations did not apply to him, he didn't have to believe me but I wouldn't waste my breath on telling lies, especially as I'd have to do it in Russian, which would be tiring. He was at liberty to believe me or not, that was up to him, but that was what I thought and it would be a good idea to put an end to the discussion.

He was intelligent. He understood I meant what I said. He put his somewhat sallow hand on mine, and said, 'I believe you.'

'It's like the titles of Soviet politicians,' I said, following my train of thought. 'They used to be called People's Commissars, and in those days it sounded right, didn't it? Then, for whatever reason, they were turned into ministers, like everywhere else. Nowadays if you tried calling them People's Commissars it would sound so peculiar.'

'If they wanted to be called People's Commissars, they'd have to start by being the commissars of the people!'

I pretended not to have heard and looked out through the window. An intermission was taking place at the cinema next to the metro station.

My conversation with Antaeus lurched on clumsily, like a caged bird beating its wings in the café until one of us managed to open the door and let it fly off to the south-eastern corner of Europe, which was home to us both. We started talking about things that had happened to us when Antaeus was a teenager and I was a child. He told me about the severed heads of Greek partisans that our enemies had kept in refrigerators to show to people, and I told him what I'd heard about the severed heads of rebellious pashas that were displayed in a stone niche in Istanbul, to dampen separatist aspirations.

'That's the way large aggressor nations always behave,' he said. 'Scare the people! Horrify them! Terrorise them mercilessly! But, tell me, what was that niche called?'

'*Ibret-taşı*: Let it be a lesson!'

'Hm.' He nodded, as a sardonic smile spread across his face. 'You share a naval base with the Soviets, don't you?'

'Yes — Pasha Liman.'

'Another Turkish name!'

Conversation drifted back to the Albanian-Greek border, to rain, winter, hail and shame.

'On the march towards Albania,' he said, 'we didn't know whether you would defend us or not. There were rumours that Tito would hand over men from our side. But you stuck to your ancient *besa* . . . *Besa*,' he whispered. 'I know that Albanian word. I heard it in Athens, when I was a student. One day it will come into every language in the world.' He stopped talking and swept his hand over the table, as if he were wiping it clean. 'OK,' he said eventually. 'Let's drop the subject. Tomorrow I shall drink like a character from an opera!'

I laughed heartily.

'Tomorrow everyone is going to get drunk. We're all at the end of our tethers . . .'

'Hanging over us all is a black cloud of discouragement,' he said, lowering his voice on the last words as if he already regretted having uttered them.

A cloud of discouragement . . . I looked through the window at the people streaming into the cinema. Most were young, holding hands or arm in arm, and all of a sudden I was overcome with joy at the memory of Lida Snegina. We'd met again since her return from Crimea and we'd been back to Neskuchny Sad, as well as to the bar on the thirteenth floor of the Peking Hotel, which had a view over all of Moscow and our other old haunts. The following day, a Sunday, we were due to meet at Novoslobodskaya metro station, and suddenly, at the table where we'd just been talking about *khandra*, thinking of Lida, I was overcome by a wave of sentimental gratitude for the metro trains that ran day and night, for overground trains, ticket-sellers, taxis that were always there to help if you were running late, and for all the other means of transport that allowed us to see each other. The warmth I experienced was such that I felt a bit of an imposter at a table where we had talked of painful things. I was about to tell Antaeus that at six thirty the next day I had an appointment with a wonderful woman at a station, but just then, without looking at me and still staring at the street, he mumbled, 'Raise your head, you faker!'

I pretended I hadn't heard and looked towards the metro station exit. I thought of Lida approaching our rendezvous the next day with the light step of any girl on her way to meet a boy, her eyes at an angle of forty-five degrees to the ground, all alone amid the passers-by, five minutes late, her steps rustling with anxiety and desire.

'Yes,' he said. 'You're perfectly right.'

I looked at him, puzzled. I hadn't grasped what he was talking about.

'A character out of comic opera,' he resumed, after a short pause. 'And yet . . .'

I still had no idea what he was talking about. 'And yet what?'

He stared at me intently. Ancient Athenian, I thought, why won't you tell me what you know?

'There's going to be a meeting in Bucharest,' he said. 'A friend of mine who's a member of the Central Committee of the Greek Party passed the information to me. You're not in the loop?'

I shrugged my shoulders. 'No!'

And it was true: I knew nothing about any meetings coming up in Bucharest or Warsaw. But if I'd heard about them I don't think I'd have been whispering and making such a drama of it as he was. There were gatherings of that kind almost every month in one or other of the socialist capitals.

'Apparently, here in Moscow as well,' he went on, in the same near-whisper, 'there's going to be a conference alongside the festivities for the anniversary of the October Revolution.'

'Really?'

'And it's already a while since they appointed the central committee and the preparatory subcommittees – the political subcommittee, the economic and cultural subcommittee . . .'

What subcommittees? Why did hearing about them make me shiver?

'Ah! You don't know anything. You didn't know that Vukmanović-Tempo has just been in Moscow as well, did you?'

'I did,' I said. 'You told me.'

'Of course. I'd forgotten.'

I was on the point of telling him what Maskiavicius had told me two days earlier about the alternately smiling and scowling faces of Khrushchev and Mao Tse-tung that had been shown on posters after their meeting a few weeks earlier in the airport at Beijing, but thought better of it. What's the point? I thought. It's probably just gossip.

He seemed about to tell me something else, or maybe not. He paused, then said, 'Tomorrow we shall drink.'

'Yes. Tomorrow,' I repeated.

While we were in the café we said the word 'tomorrow' many times in a particular way, almost with a kind of relief. Occasionally it seemed to me – and maybe to Antaeus as well – that we were piling into it, as into a dustbin, all our unexpressed thoughts, all our hopes, our flaws and our mutual suspicions.

★

Sometimes Sunday seemed so palpable to me that I almost believed it was embossed and in colour. I could even feel it moving and sliding away under our skis, beneath our feet. I felt as if in this endlessly white and undulating area it had always been Sunday, since the time of the tsars and even further back, that it had been Sunday since the year 1407 or 1007. How many times had Mondays, Wednesdays, Saturdays and even savage Tuesdays come close? They'd prowled around silently in the hope of getting on to the plateau – to no avail. They eventually understood there was no easy way in for them and had discreetly withdrawn from an area where Sunday had reigned supreme for centuries.

Grey *izba*s dotted the landscape beneath a uniform sky about which I had written a hendecasyllabic line some time before: *The formless sky is like an idiot's brain*. In Russian translation it sounded even more grisly:

Безформенное неъо как мозг тупици
Унылый дождь заливает улицы

I'd been harshly criticised for it in the poetry seminar.

The day was rushing away beneath my feet. Among the hummocks of snow, people with odd fixtures on their skis came and went, then dropped in at the Writers' Club and reappeared with greater ease in their movements, having downed a dram without even taking off their skis.

In fact, with a few exceptions, nobody knew how to ski properly, but none of us ever took our skis off. Taburokov even tried to go to the toilet with his on.

They all looked drunk. But it wasn't just the vodka. They

were under the influence of the uninterrupted sky, the sadness of the horizontal beams of the *izba*s, and the snow, which made it so easy to laugh (Kurganov said that only in snow can people laugh one hundred per cent, especially if their feet are strapped into skis).

We spent the whole day going round in unending circles, with the hissing sound of skiers lost on the *piste*, disappearing then reappearing from behind mounds of snow, like ungainly ghosts.

At twilight the intoxication increased. But that was only the beginning. The tacit understanding was that everything would happen 'at our place', the hall of residence at Butyrsky Khutor.

Night fell, and our noisy party set off for the railway station, full of expectation and foreboding. The floor of the carriage was soon dotted with clumps of snow. As we got on, passengers stared at us, their curiosity tinged with disapproval. There were women from the outlying regions with knapsacks in their laps, a girl and a boy with colourless hair, clenched fists and hooligans' scars on their rough cheeks. The latest fashion among teenage ruffians was to put blades between their knuckles so even the slightest blow would draw blood.

The train juddered into motion. The familiar landscape slid backwards at an increasing rate. My idea of an everlasting Sunday vanished. No, at Peredelkino it was never Sunday or Thursday, it was only ever today. Eternally now. Sunday was what we had brought to it, like roast lamb to a picnic, like the savages had brought Friday to Robinson Crusoe's island. We'd brought our Moscow Sunday so we could cope with it in peace, between the *izba*s and the sky, far from other human eyes.

Now everything was over and dusk had fallen. Small suburban stations rushed past. Alcoholic fumes befuddled our sense of proportion. Outside in the snowy landscape we glimpsed people wrapped from head to toe in angora houpelandes, as if they had just walked out of a Russian folktale. A group of young people got on. With them were two girls, pink with cold, who gazed at everything as if they were under the influence. The Shotas stared at them.

'*Simpatiaga*,' one of the girls said, referring to a Shota.

I'd never heard the suffix -*iaga* added to the Russian word for 'nice': it usually expressed disdain or referred to ugliness.

Behind me I heard 'Masses in Their Tens of Millions' saying to Abdullakhanov: 'You understand, Khrushchev spent three days in the country as Sholokhov's house-guest . . .'

Abdullakhanov clicked his tongue against the roof of his mouth. 'Tut-tut. If anyone else had told me I wouldn't have believed it, but since it comes from you, I'll take you at your word.'

'But it's serious!' Pogosian retorted. 'I heard it on the radio.'

'Ha! On the radio! On the radio!' Abdullakhanov repeated, nodding so vigorously that it seemed he was banging his head against the window.

Further down the carriage, Taburokov was standing still but was shaken, at regular intervals, by hiccups, which made him roll his eyes, as if he was watching an insect fluttering at the end of his nose.

'A three-day stay,' 'Masses in Their Tens of Millions' went on, just behind my neck. 'The peasant drops in on the peasant . . . Ssh! . . . while the noble Armenian people . . . did I say anything? . . . bask in happiness!'

I changed my seat so that I wouldn't hear Pogosian raving in his medley of Russian and Armenian and found myself opposite Shakenov, who was reciting for the benefit of one of the 'Belarusian Virgins' his recently completed 'The March of the Savings Banks'. Three months previously he had published 'The March of the Soviet Law Courts', which had brought him sacks of readers' letters. 'All you have to do now,' Stulpanc had joked, 'is to write "The March of the Soviet Prisoners", but you've got plenty of time, you never know what might happen.'

'A three-day stay! My God! We're back to the days of the Russian peasantry. But mum's the word!'

Artashez Pogosian had wriggled closer to me again and this time there was no escape. The carriage hummed with whispers and mumbling. I reckoned they had probably begun to pour out their hearts and entrust each other with the subjects of the plays and novels they had written or planned to write. It was customary after serious drinking. On the way back from Yalta the previous winter, throughout the long train trip across the lush Ukrainian countryside, standing in the slippery corridor of the carriage, which often smelt of vomit, I'd heard endless tales of that kind, all night long, whole chapters of novels, entire acts from plays. But the journey from Peredelkino to Moscow was short and there wasn't sufficient time.

The Shotas had tried but failed to engage the two girls

in conversation. I looked around for Antaeus but all I found was the pasty, fish-eyed face of the art history professor. She was a well-known iconographer, and I suddenly realised that, despite the icon-like pallor and flatness of her face, she was still a young woman. I moved closer to her, and she asked me sweetly, 'Don't you have your own story to tell?'

I was taken aback. 'To whom?'

'To me, of course!'

Her eyes seemed like part of a very old painting, worn away by time.

'But my story is about dead people,' I said. 'My subject—'

'OK,' she said. 'What's wrong with that?'

Of course, there was nothing wrong with it. It occurred to me that, with the way she looked, the only subjects anyone would ever want to broach would be macabre.

'Maybe I'll tell you later, in Moscow, when we're back,' I said.

'As you wish,' she said. 'I can wait.'

I could barely repress a shudder. What exactly was she expecting? I turned to look out of the window but the darkness had swallowed everything. It was completely black outside. A black abyss, with us moving blindly through it. It was nearly six and I thought I would miss my appointment with Lida at the Novoslobodskaya metro station. Oddly, that did not upset me. If only you knew, Lida! I thought placidly. But on the heels of that thought came another: what was it precisely that Lida should know? Nothing. A suburban railway carriage, a wet floor and, trodden into the still only half-melted clumps of snow, stories that would never be written and theatrical scenarios that would never be performed on any stage . . .

We got to Moscow around seven. Our group made a bois- terous entrance at the Gorky Institute. Most of us were swaying on our feet, wearing innocent smiles and burping occasionally.

'Ah! Here are my lambs, returning to the fold,' said Auntie Katya, from behind her counter.

Meanwhile, those who had stayed behind at the residence came out into the corridor or opened their doors to welcome the travellers home. But they looked much the same as the returning mob. The vast building was full of grating voices, snatches of song, vodka fumes and the banging of toilet doors. I tramped along corridors on various floors until, in a dark corner, there loomed before me the black shape of a public telephone with the digits on its dial gleaming as white as shark's teeth. Lida had surely gone home upset and angry. I put fifteen kopecks' worth of coins into the slot and dialled. 'Hello!' she said. Yes, she was cross, but calm. I tried to persuade her it wasn't my fault, but to judge by her curt and haughty response, she must have been waiting for me to hang up. I told her we could meet at the same place a little later, but she refused. I'd almost lost all hope of seeing her again and felt dreadful.

'Lida,' I said, my voice cracking, 'I really need to see you this evening. If you knew . . .'

'If I knew what?' she asked. Her voice had perked up, grown lighter and sharper in the huge, still midnight space where you think you can hear stars bumping into each other. 'What?' she asked again.

'If you knew how horrible it is here tonight . . .'

The midnight void settled between us, like the emptiness of a morgue. Then she asked: 'Are you lonely?'

'Yes,' I answered faintly. I would have liked to add words of a kind that has never existed. For a split second I thought I knew some but I didn't move my lips to say them aloud. I just sighed. It was such a sigh that I imagined that if I didn't get a grip on myself right now my very soul would be ready to depart my body.

'All right,' she said. 'I'll come. Wait for me at the usual place.'

I ran to the trolleybus stop and twenty minutes later I was at the metro station. The escalators spewed out an endless stream of travellers. Their astonishingly fixed heads came out first, then their chests and finally their legs. I felt confused. I was afraid I stank to high heaven of vodka. Sometimes I even imagined I still had my skis on. At last I saw her golden hair appear with its electric sparkle, then her neck, so straight, the memory of which was always accompanied by a kind of pain. In my mind the idea of losing Lida was always associated with a vision of that straight neck alongside someone else's.

'Here I am,' she said, without a smile.

Her inquisitive eyes looked me up and down from head to toe. We'd become strangers. Only when she took off her gloves to pick something off my shoulder, maybe a snow-flake, did she seem close again.

We walked for a little while in the wake of the moving crowd.

'Have you been drinking?' she asked.

'No . . . I mean . . . only a little,' I mumbled. 'You know I don't like drinking.'

'So, at your place, is it really as dreadful as you said?' She wasn't looking at me.

'Yes, yes, back there it's sheer hell.'

She shrugged.

'Would you like to come and see?' I asked.

'I don't know.'

I felt I wasn't making myself clear, which made me want to take her there.

We were going past the gloomy walls of Butyrky Prison when she exclaimed: 'Look! There's a taxi!'

We hailed it and, without thinking what I was doing, I gave the driver the address of the Gorky Institute hall of residence.

I could see lights twinkling in the building. A knot of tipsy students were talking to each other in front of the porter's lodge. Auntie Katya had livened up, too. On party nights when residents had been drinking they were usually quite open-handed as well. She was talking with Taburokov and laughing, but when she saw me her face suddenly darkened. Her narrow eyes with their reddish lashes cut through Lida like a knife.

'Your ID, my girl.'

Lida was flustered. She looked in her bag, then at me. I didn't know what to say.

'Haven't you got some kind of card?' I whispered. 'It's just a formality.'

The old hag never asked for papers from the dozens of

girls who came into our residence with their boyfriends. She had only been doing it to me for the last few weeks, undoubtedly because of the police summons.

Lida scrabbled in her handbag again and fished out a card.

'Ah!' said Auntie Katya, as she studied it. 'A Komsomol card. Hm!'

You old witch! I thought. *Baba Yaga!*

But Kurganov came to my help and asked her outright, 'Why are you asking for ID from his friends? You never ask anyone else.'

'You keep your mouth shut!' Auntie Katya riposted. 'This is management business.'

Lida's mood had darkened.

'Yes, why is she so keen to see the IDs of your friends?' she asked, as we waited for the lift.

I shrugged.

'Does she think you're a suspicious character?' she pressed.

I still didn't know what to say so I shrugged again. 'I'm a foreigner.'

She stared at me for a moment, then looked away. But in her eyes, for an instant, I thought I saw something like compassion. Infinite compassion in a halo of light, quite different from the ordinary human kind. I was well aware that, amid the hostility between males that blanketed everything like winter, Russian girls had the courage to protect foreign guests.

How difficult it is to get into foreign lifts . . . But we got in. As it slid upwards, the iron fretwork of the shaft allowed glimpses of corridors on various floors, room numbers, faces and necks. I tried to tell Lida about the residence and its inmates. First floor: that's where the first-year students stay; they've not yet committed many literary sins. Second floor: critics, conformist playwrights, white-washers. Third . . . circle: dogmatics, arse-lickers and Russian nationalists. Fourth circle: women, liberals, and people disenchanted with socialism. Fifth circle: slanderers and snitches. Sixth circle: denaturalised writers who have abandoned their own language to write in Russian . . .

That was where the lift came to a halt, on the sixth floor. As I opened the door I bumped into Stulpanc who, for no obvious reason, just stood there, stock still, apparently stunned.

'Denaturalised . . .' she echoed. 'So you're one of those who's abandoned his own language?'

'No, not me. I'm a foreigner.'

Stulpanc fixed his pale eyes on Lida.

'This Latvian hasn't yet renounced his own tongue either,' I whispered in her ear, 'but they're working on him.'

'What a beauty!' Stulpanc said of Lida, without shifting his gaze.

He was a serious young man and I'd never seen him behave like that before. But that night, drink had got the better of him.

There was a strange excitement in the corridor. You could feel that something was afoot. I thought I could distinguish a group of Karakums huddling somewhere near my room. As Lida and I approached, the group vanished. All I found were the two Shotas emerging from the service staircase and swearing at each other. One was tall and fat-faced, his cheeks even more florid than usual; the other was a short, sly customer, who looked like a ball of wool. Hardship and resentment seemed to have settled in his thick hair, curling and frizzling it into a nest.

Lida took my arm and held it tight.

A sad Asian song came from behind a door. Further down we caught fragments of sentences in languages we'd never heard before.

'Let's get out,' Lida said. 'Why did you bring me here?'

'We'll go down to the fourth floor. Perhaps they've started the outpouring.'

'What's that?'

'Plot-spew! That's what they call it. On nights like this they tell each other the plots of books they'll never write. Some of them throw up – that's why they call these sessions plot-spews.'

'How can you say such horrible things?'

'Let's go downstairs,' I said. 'You'll see for yourself.'

On our way we met Goncharov going up.

'He's a government spy,' I told Lida.

'From the fifth floor?'

'What a good memory you've got!'

She clutched me tighter. On the fourth floor the outpourings had indeed already begun. In pairs, rarely in threes, my fellows slowly paced from door to door in the ill-lit parts of the corridor, mumbling as they went. Plot-spews were still few but the distraught expressions on their faces made it clear there would soon be plenty.

'They'll never write any of the things they'll tell each other about tonight,' I explained to Lida. 'They'll write other things, often the exact opposite.'

'That's why I don't like writers. How fortunate you are not to be one of them!' She added, as an afterthought, 'Please, don't crack your fingers like that!'

In a muddle, I got out my handkerchief and spat into it.

She looked at me, appalled. 'What's come over you? You never do that.'

'What do you mean?'

'That. Spitting like that.'

'I've no idea if I do or I don't . . .' I really didn't know what had got into me.

'Why do you live here? Can't you find somewhere else?'

I shrugged my shoulders.

'Ladonshchikov is a bastard,' somebody shouted, leaning on his door.

From the end of the corridor of the women's floor came sounds of music.

Lida stopped dead. On the floor, at her feet, was a puddle. It looked like vomit and probably was.

'I'd say that was playwright's spew,' I joked.

'Stop it! Please, let's get out of here.'

We took the stairs. Maskiavicius, whose nose was bleeding, overtook us. I wanted to say hello but Lida tugged at my sleeve.

'What's the matter with you?' I asked her.

She sighed deeply. 'What's the matter with *you*?' she replied. 'You're like a bear with a sore head.'

I was on edge. I had an almost irresistible urge to do just about anything or, rather, to undo something. My knees felt out of joint, my elbows felt dislocated, my jaw felt unhinged. I tasted ash.

'What's up?' she said. 'You're hurting my arm!'

I jerked my head around to look at her with almost hate-filled eyes. That was why I couldn't control myself this evening. It was because of her. She was the reason my nerves were in such a state – she and her face, with its halo of solar wisps, her purity and propriety, with the white obelisk of her neck, defying everything around it, including me. Right! I thought, in a moment of lunacy. You'll soon see what I'm really like! An irresistible desire to hurt her tightened into a ball inside my chest.

'What is wrong with you?' Her voice was softer now. She was gazing at me with sympathy, clouded with a bluish haze. 'What's wrong?' she asked again.

You'll soon see, you little witch!

We were on the sixth floor and I was leaning against the lift-cage ironwork. She saw that I was about to tell her something important; she was waiting for it with her mouth half open and what might have been the marks of suffering on her cheeks.

'Listen!' I said, in a feeble voice I could barely get past my teeth. Then, my eyes darting around as if I was about to reveal a great secret, I mumbled something half Albanian and half Russian that I didn't understand myself.

She looked at me serenely. Then, putting a hand on my shoulder, she drew her head close to mine as if she had spotted something barely visible in the depths of my eyes, at the back of my skull. Hoarsely, as if she'd said, 'From now on you are a diminished man in my eyes, you are a murderer, a member of the Mafia, of the Zionist International, of the Ku Klux Klan,' she whispered, 'I'm beginning to believe that you . . . you too . . . you are a writer!'

It seemed to me that my answer was just a laugh. 'Yes,' I said. 'I am a writer but, unfortunately, not a dead one!'

We stood there for a while just looking each other in the eye.

'I'd started thinking you were,' she murmured.

Suddenly I felt that my confession had not been destructive enough and I hastened to finish digging myself into a hole. I told her that if I didn't get out soon I would start throwing up as the others did, not just in the corridor but from the windows on to passers-by, on to taxis, from the sixth floor, from the top of the Kremlin's towers, from – from—

Her eyes were popping as she put one hand over her mouth and, with the other, pressed the call button for the lift. Eventually it arrived but only when she closed the door on herself did I grasp that she was leaving. I shook the handle but it was already on its way down. I started running down the stairs, winding round and round the cage inside which Lida was falling, inexorably falling. I spiralled around a void that was a monumental column. I clung to it as though I were an ornament, in classical, Doric, Ionian or Corinthian style, wrapped around Trajan's column, crisscrossing the bas-relief depictions of battles, armour, blood, and horses with hoofs that trampled my head . . .

When I got to the bottom the lift's door was open and it was empty. Lida had gone. I saw Stulpanc pacing up and down the corridor.

'I saw your girlfriend,' he said. 'Why was she in such a hurry to get out?'

I mumbled a few incomprehensible syllables.

'What a fabulous girl!' he added. 'You're a fool to let her go.'

'If you want her, take her!'

His eyes widened.

What made me rejoice in the satisfaction of revenge? Oh, yes. In saying 'Take her!' to Stulpanc, I had maintained the illusion that I was treating her like a harem slave, selling her on. I knew it wasn't true, that I had no power over her, but the brash way in which I'd offered her to Stulpanc made me feel as if I had.

In fact, the previous year, at a very private party in his room, when we had been drunk, we had swapped partners. It was an episode neither of us liked to recall.

'She's all yours,' I repeated. 'I'm serious. Over to you.'

'Hang on,' said Stulpanc. 'Tell me more . . .'

'There's no deal involved,' I told him. 'She's a present.'

Absurdly, I felt relieved.

'But how am I going to—'

'Look, here's her phone number,' I said, fishing a piece of paper out of my pocket. 'Call her some evening and tell her I've left or gone mad or— Wait . . . say I'm dead! Do you hear? Tell her I died in a plane crash.'

The idea that if she believed I was dead she would think of me with affection, perhaps even love, flashed through my mind and something softened in my chest.

Stulpanc stared at me, astonished. 'No,' he said after a pause. 'I don't like the way you're behaving.' And he gave me back the scrap of paper with her phone number.

'Go on!' I said. 'I've lost her anyway. I'd rather it was you who laid her next instead of an Eskimo or some Uzbek pimp.'

I turned my back and made for the stairs. There was dancing on one of the lower floors. My last words to Stulpanc had been entirely sincere. Through a glass door I could see the outlines of couples dancing. Now and again I thought of Lida walking alone across Moscow. It's cold outside, I thought, as I got to the Russian-nationalist floor. It's pitch black out there and the streets are full of Tatars . . . And now you're writing ballads!

On the fourth floor I fell in with the disenchanted, who were whispering to each other as they paced up and down, two by two. Maybe it was the narrowness of the corridor that made them seem taller than they were in the Institute's lecture theatres. But maybe the disenchanted always seem taller than they are . . . Fragments of scenes and synopses, spoken in more or less muffled tones, reached my ears, sometimes the left, at others the right. Themes ranged from limping party secretaries who stole piglets from the collective farm, fake ministers, decrepit and dim-witted generals, and Politburo members who spied on each other and buried a proportion of their pay under *izba* floors against a rainy day. Some stories portrayed top officials' luxurious *dacha*s, their drinking parties and bribes, and their offspring dancing in the nude. Others dealt with uprisings, if not with real insurrections in various parts of the country; they spoke of hushed-up massacres, the growth of religious sects, deportation, prisons and crimes, the monstrous difference in pay between workers, the supposed 'masters of the land', and the leading cadres of the Party and state, 'the people's servants'. '*A Hundred to One* is the title of my play,' said a voice. 'Maybe you think I'm telling a story about a Soviet soldier fighting off a hundred Germans, a revolutionary overcoming a hundred Tsarists, or a Korean versus a hundred Americans. No, my sweet, there's nothing of the sort in my play. A hundred to one means that the salary of one character is a hundred times higher than that of another, and what's most amazing about it is that they're both positive characters!'

'Ha-ha-ha!' said his interlocutor.

'Yes, yes, my play ends just like that, with a laugh,' the playwright replied. 'My low-paid character starts giggling, ha-ha-ha! The whole company bursts out laughing, ha-ha-ha!, and the laughter spreads to the audience and from the audience it ignites the whole wintry city. And then all that's left for Piotr Ivanovich is a wee stretch of time in our cosy little prison at Butyrky!'

'Ha-ha!' said the other.

'Yuri Goncharov!' someone said. In the blink of an eye, the novels, plays and poems metamorphosed. The tall, sturdy Party Secretary gives his jacket to a comrade feeling the cold; the Party committee delegate, seen in Act I of version A distilling vodka illegally, now forgets to draw his pay, forgets even to have dinner because he is so absorbed by world revolution; insurrections are transformed into art fairs on collective farms, massacres recast as prize-giving ceremonies; youngsters who danced naked in *dacha*s now volunteer to upturn the virgin soil. Whereupon the disenchanted all began to throw up . . .

I turned and plunged blindly into the other part of the

corridor where the women lived. There was a bitter taste in my mouth. Outside one door I thought I recognised the 'Belarusian Virgins', and a little further on, the haughty expression and eternal cigarette of their antithesis, Bella Akhmadulina, Yevgeny Yevtushenko's wife. She was in her fourth year. With a complexion that was milk-white, despite her Tatar ancestry and good health, she exuded impending maternity, which she never mentioned in her poetry. Each time I met her on the stairs, I could not help thinking of the efforts she must have made to be dressed always at the height of fashion.

'*Bon akşam*, Bella,' I muttered, through my teeth.

'. . . *akşam*,' she breathed, without taking the cigarette out of her mouth.

Nobody knew who had invented this half-French, half-Turkish 'good evening', but almost everyone had adopted it. *Akşam*, I repeated inwardly without ceasing to gaze at Bella's pale face, sadness rippling across it, like waves on a pond. Melancholy clung to the mascara on her eyelashes and spread over the Saharan expanse of the shimmering, moon-like powder on her neck. *Akşam*, I thought. What a majestic word! This evening is truly an *akşam*. It's not an *Abend* or a *soir* or a вечер, but an *akşam*. Let *akşam* reign on the frozen steppes of Russia, on the phone lines of the night shift, in the cities and collective farms, over the memories of the civil war, over snow, guns and the soviets of the sixteen republics. *Akşam* be upon the vastest state in the world!

That was when I saw our professor of art history. She was standing at the very end of the corridor, almost glued to the wall, and her eyes were trained on me.

'I'm still waiting,' said the icon, barely audible.

I stopped in my tracks and glared at my boots.

'You promised me a plot,' the wall-bound voice went on. 'A plot with death in it.'

I moved a step nearer. Her face was close to mine now. She had pale skin and unhealthy pink blotches on both cheeks. 'With death in it,' I repeated, as if I had heard my own sentence read out. I leaned even nearer and, very gently, not even putting my hand on her unflinching shoulders, I kissed her on the lips. Then I drew my head back in the same measured way, as if expecting the human mural to crumble and bury me in its rubble. I took a few steps backwards. Then, without a pause, I turned on my heels and ran down the corridor.

'Oh, those bloody Chinese!' I heard someone say, as he peered through the keyhole of Ping's door. 'Come on, Hundred Flower Bloom, or Hundred Nettles, whatever your name is! You there, you inside, open up! I've got something to tell you . . .' Not a sound came from within.

'Ladonshchikov is a turd!' another voice wailed, but I didn't turn to see whose it was. I ran up the stairs four by four and was gasping for breath by the time I got to the sixth floor. The first person I fell upon was Taburokov. With his wispy black hair rising from his sweaty scalp, like fumes from the flame of a gas hob, he came towards me like an apparition in blue. '*Nkell gox avahl uhr*,' he said threateningly, but I evaded him and went past.

'A Mongolian has jumped out of a window on the fifth floor,' someone said. 'Call Emergency!'

Despite the dim lighting there was muffled excitement

along the corridor. Denaturalised writers were coming and
going in disarray amid suppressed quarrelling. Now and
again dull thuds could be heard. Boom! Boom! That must
have been Abdullakhanov banging his head against the wall,
as he usually did after more than two hours' drinking.
Nearby I heard mumbling: '*Hran, xingeth frull ckellfirau hie.*'
It came from the Karakums, advancing in a squad from the
depths of the corridor. They were speaking their own half-
dead language and their words whistled past me, like a
sandstorm desiccated by the desert sun. '*Auhr, auhr, nkr ub
. . .*' I wanted to get out, to get away from the dust that
was already grating on my teeth and coating me with its
namelessness. I fell, my friends, I fell, *krauhl ah rk meit!* On
the other side of the bridge at Mecca . . . Fortunately I
found myself at the opening of the unlit corridor that led
on my right towards the empty suite, and I plunged into
it. As I went along it in a state of bewilderment I heard a
noise that sounded like the rustling of reeds against a gurgle
of water. I thought my feet were sinking into mud, my
legs were unsteady, I was about to be swallowed by soggy
tundra. Kyuzengesh had sprung up beside me. '*Bon akşam,*'
I whispered.

'*Jounalla hanelle avuksi,*' he replied.

I'd never heard the sound of his voice before. As he carried
on speaking I tried to hang on to the wall so that I didn't
sink into the mud. Although he had always seemed placid
and slightly bemused, he was now talking harshly, if still at
low volume. His anger was easier to see than to hear. You
could read the fury in his crooked teeth – they looked like
whitish blobs emitting words of death, or small tombstones

half buried in a muddy pit. I turned my back on him and found myself once again in the sixth-floor corridor where the denaturalised group was now thoroughly mixed up and speaking all its dead and dying languages simultaneously. It was a dreadful nightmare. Their greasy faces distorted by drink and sweat, and streaked with dried tears, they were hoarsely espousing the languages they had rejected, beating their breasts, sobbing and swearing they would never forget them, they would speak them in their dreams; they were castigating themselves for having abandoned their languages, their mother tongues, for having left them at home to the mercy of mountains or deserts so they could take up with that hag of a stepmother, Russian.

I was struck dumb. I'd never imagined I would witness repentance on such a grand scale. '*Meilla ubr*,' I said, I've no idea why.

They wittered on. In the word soup of already dead and gravely sick languages, a few Russian expressions floated to the surface. They cropped up like lost islands in the dark ocean of a collective subconscious. 'I can see my language before me, like a ghost!' one kept screaming, as if he had just woken up in fright. *Frulldjek, frulldjek hain. Ikunlukut uha olalla.* Fuck off. *Ah onc kllxg buhu. Meit aham*, without a horse or so much as a farewell. This autumn, *tuuli lakamata*. O star! *Vulldiz, et, hakr bil*, O my language!

You won't be able to say I did it! Oh, stop dangling your blood-stained suffixes over me!

Stop! I thought. I stuffed my fingers into my ears, struggled to make my way through the group and eventually got to my room. I flung myself straight on to my bed

without taking my hands from my ears. What kind of
country is this? And why am I in it? I couldn't think further
than that. I wanted to cry but I couldn't. My chest went
into a kind of convulsion once or twice, but it was a dry
sob.

CHAPTER FOUR

'Doctor, Doctor, help me! I'm feeling very bad . . . Ah! Dr Zhivago, Dr Zhivago . . . The bastard!'

What's happening? I wondered, in my sleep, as I snuggled deeper under my blankets. Who's calling for a doctor and how did he get into my room? My mind was still befuddled from the previous night and I wasn't up to understanding anything much. Someone was feeling ill, doubtless because of last night's drunken binge. Maybe it was Stulpanc, or one of the Karakums, asking for a doctor to help. To hell with them! I thought. I'm not a doctor and they've no reason to yell at me through the keyhole like that. I stuffed a loose corner of blanket into my ear and tried to get back to sleep, but it didn't work. Someone went on calling for help, moaning and uttering indirect threats. You really should go to hell, I thought. You drank like a fish all night, and now you want help? I stuffed my head between the pillows and tried to go to sleep but I could feel the voice calling me, obstinately and evenly. What makes him think I'm a doctor? I wondered in my half-awake state. 'Doctor, Doctor!' Enough! After a night like that, I could really do without this! I threw off my bedclothes and listened hard. It was a strange voice, which took a couple of seconds to shake itself free of the aural fog that had shrouded it in my half-conscious mind. It emerged different – unadorned, firm, inhuman: '. . . the bourgeoisie's nefarious aims, this infamous anti-Soviet work. Boris Pasternak's *Doctor Zhivago* is the expression of . . .'

Only then did I realise I had forgotten to switch off my radio when I'd gone to bed. I tried to raise myself to hear it better but my head was still too leaden. The announcer was going on angrily about some novel about a doctor. Dr Zhivago, Dr Zhivago . . . Where had I seen or heard that name before? Oh, yes! In the empty apartment, of course: still-life with sardine tin and typescript. The announcer was probably fulminating against that very script. At first I felt like laughing: a typescript and an empty vodka bottle! Were they really worth air time on Radio Moscow so early in the morning?

'. . . a provocative and odious action of the international bourgeoisie. The award of the Nobel Prize to this reactionary novel . . .'

I whistled. This was serious. A novel called *Doctor Zhivago* had bagged the Nobel. It had to be a bad novel. A very bad one! Appalling, even!

I held my neck stiff, as if it had been screwed to the pillow, to listen to the rest of the broadcast. It was a gloomy morning. A greyish light strained to get through the double-glazed windows and barely allowed me to make out what was in the room. It was grey and drab, save for the dimly lit rectangle of the radio, whence emanated words that were just as sombre and sticky: '. . . the peoples of the Soviet

Union . . . indignant . . . libellous . . . scurrilous . . . This counter-revolutionary novel . . . our magnificent Soviet reality . . . dragged through the mud . . .'

Could those typed pages beside the bottle and empty tin really contain all those abominations? I'd held them in my hand without suspecting a thing. But who had written them? I thought I'd heard the name Boris Pasternak. I put out an ear. Yes, that was it. Now his name was being repeated every three to four seconds. How odd. I'd seen Pasternak less than two months previously on a walk in the woods around Peredelkino. We'd left the village and Maskiavicius had pointed out Pasternak's *dacha* to me. It was a large two-storey cottage with big bay windows on the ground floor. 'Look, there he is!' Maskiavicius had said, a few moments later, pointing to the grounds of the villa. I'd gone up to the fence. At 'heart-pouring' times I'd often heard his name mentioned – with admiration from some, but hatred from others – and I was curious to see him, a few feet away from me, digging the garden outside his *dacha*. He was wearing a very plain cap and boots and, with his strong jaw, he looked like the vice-president of a collective farm.

'Assuming the role of an agent of the international bourgeoisie, Boris Pasternak . . .'

A Nobel Prize didn't seem compatible in my eyes with the rolled-up sleeves of the shirt he'd obviously bought from the store at the nearest *kolkhoz* . . .

I got up, dressed, and went into the corridor. In the half-light I could see people dotted around, but they were almost unrecognisable with their swollen eyes, and they seemed to find it hard to recognise anyone else. It was half past eight and most of the residents were still asleep. I was tempted to go back to the empty suite to have another look at that accursed typescript, but I thought better of it straight away. Why should I get into an extra tangle with the KGB now that I was sure Auntie Katya had been ordered to demand the papers of anyone visiting me? The communal bathrooms where we washed every morning were deserted. The cleaners had dealt with the vomit, and not a trace of it remained: everything was clean and cold. I took a look at myself in the mirror. I had big bags under my eyes, my right eye was swollen, as if I'd broken a blood vessel, and my complexion was earthen. If Lida had seen me she would have believed I really was dead! Immediately I felt a needle stuck into my heart: Lida in the lift . . . Trajan's column . . . her telephone number handed over to Stulpanc . . . What a fool! I said to myself. I must be the king of cretins to do that!

As I was crossing Pushkin Square on my way to the Institute, I noticed that people queuing for tickets at the Central Cinema were deeply absorbed in their newspapers. That must mean the press has started its campaign, I thought.

The wind was cold, with something blind and unforgiving about it. I crossed Gorky Street at the junction, went into the pharmacy on the other side and bought some aspirin, then hurried on – I didn't want to be late for my lecture.

The professor had just come into the lecture hall. I pushed the door open very quietly, and when I entered, I noticed the room was almost empty. It was very dark and

I wondered why nobody had put the lights on. Was there a power cut? I could make out two shapes near the windows and a third in a corner; maybe it was Shogentsukov.

The lecturer looked at his watch, brought his wrist closer to his eyes to make out the time, then looked around as if to ask, 'What's going on?' Half out of his briefcase, I saw a morning paper with Pasternak's name on the front page.

I soon recognised one of the shapes near the window: it was Antaeus. The other one, in the corner, was indeed Shogentsukov. He never missed the first lecture of the day: it was a habit, as he said, that he'd adopted when he was prime minister and held meetings with his cabinet at seven in the morning. Now he was hunkered down in the corner as if he had turned to stone.

The door swung open and the 'Belarusian Virgins' made their entrance, with Yuri Goncharov behind them. They were all holding a copy of *Literaturnaya gazeta*, the organ of the Writers' Union. Then, on the threshold of the lecture hall, the plump, solemn and drab figure of Ladonshchikov appeared.

'Morning, comrades,' he said, in a peculiar voice that seemed to combine a sigh and a threat, concern for the common cause and mournful meditation, executive emotion and the gnashing of teeth.

As they came in each one flicked the light switch and, after looking either at the ceiling fixture or at the lectern, mumbled something about there being no power. Ladonshchikov did likewise, then slumped into his seat and opened his newspaper. '*Vot podlets!* What a scoundrel!' he barked, after a while. His face and the unfolded newspaper then engaged in a curious mirror-dance: his eyebrows moved in lock-step with the headlines, his lips responded and his teeth ground in harmony with the printed words.

The lecturer had begun. It was already half past nine but the hall was still in deep twilight. Daylight from the windows cast illumination only as far down as the print of a Repin picture hanging on the wall opposite me. I'd never even read the caption on the painting, which showed a few wooden faces belonging to high officials or to the editorial board of a journal that would never appear, or perhaps they were a military high command that had never gone to war and never would. Any time you were feeling depressed, that picture made your mood even darker.

'What happened to you?' Antaeus asked me, in the break. 'What's that graze on your forehead?'

I put my hand to my head and discovered that it was a bit sore. 'I don't know!'

I really didn't. Maybe I'd scratched it on the lift cage – or had somebody done it with their nails?

'Did the drinking go on late last night?'

'Don't bring that up.'

Antaeus lived on his own in an apartment on Neglinnaya Street and had not yet caught up with what had gone on at the hall of residence.

'You've heard about the Pasternak affair?'

I nodded. There was a sarcastic gleam in his intelligent eyes.

The rest of the group slowly trickled in. Pale and dishevelled, some looking grey as steel, others with puffy cheeks and narrowed eyes, a few more simply haggard, they burst into the hallway and took off their heavy winter coats. They were all holding a newspaper in one hand. In the state they were in, it was surprising their eyes were still capable of deciphering a headline, let alone an article. It struck me that any normally constituted individual would have shivered with dread on seeing them all loom up like that. They looked as though they had torn their eyes out during a night of tormented sleep, thrown them at random on top of their discarded clothes, and on waking this morning, had fumbled around to find them, stuck them back in any old how, then dashed, squinting, to the Institute.

The next lecture was on art history.

As we trooped back into the hall, the lecturer came up to me and smiled brightly.

'Your topic was just wonderful,' she said.

'What topic?' I replied, almost scared. 'I haven't prepared anything.'

She went on smiling. 'A living army commanded by the ghosts of a dead general and a dead priest. A fantastic invention!'

'No, that's not it,' I murmured, though I had no wish to elucidate. 'It's more like the other way round. A dead army commanded by a living general and a living priest.'

'Really?' she said, tipping her head to one side, while I racked my brains, trying to remember when I had told her about it. I had no recall. 'But that's even better,' she went on. 'I think it's even more beautiful. Are you aware of the Pasternak business?'

'Yes.'

She began her lecture, but nobody was paying attention. Minds were elsewhere.

At the next break most students went outside. The courtyard was packed and there was much more excitement than usual. Everybody, from first-year students to seniors, postgraduates and professors, was holding an open or read and refolded copy of *Literaturnaya gazeta*. Some were reading *Pravda* or *Izvestia*, both of which carried front-page attacks on Pasternak. One of the Shotas had an economics magazine that also denounced Pasternak on its front page.

Nobody talked about anything else. Some spoke harshly, others more timidly. The Nobel Prize? 'Out, damned spot! Out, I say!' A Scandinavian plague. 'Even though Sholokhov takes a trip to Sweden every year to make sure the Academicians haven't forgotten about him?' someone behind me blurted out.

'Keep your voice down!' a friend warned. 'You talk too much!'

'What is the Nobel Prize, then?' Taburokov asked one of the 'Belarusian Virgins'. 'I must have heard something about it . . .'

'A poisoned gift of the international bourgeoisie,' she explained.

'And what does that old running-dog Ilya Ehrenburg say about the business?' Maskiavicius mumbled behind me. He seemed to be looking for someone to talk to. I kept clear of him as discreetly as I could but, after he'd exchanged a few words with people I barely knew, he decided to launch into Ping, the Chinese student.

'What do you think of Pasternak?'

Hundred Flower Bloom stared at him in bewilderment.

Maskiavicius asked him a couple more questions but Ping did not open his lips. Then Maskiavicius swore at him. Apparently Ping didn't grasp the meaning because, as soon as Maskiavicius had turned his back, he pulled a concise dictionary from his pocket and started leafing through it, as he always did when he heard a word he did not know.

Somebody switched on a transistor. Yet more on Pasternak.

'Looks like the campaign is being conducted throughout the length and breadth of the Soviet Union,' I said to Antaeus.

'It's a joke. A farce.'

'Why so?'

He looked around, then lowered his voice and whispered, 'Do you remember the ballad by Goethe where someone calls on the spirits to help him fetch water from a well and then can't get rid of them?'

We'd already had a conversation about that. For some time nothing had been heard from either Stalin's supporters or his detractors. The state had been reassuring each side alternately so it could turn on either without warning.

At the moment it seemed to be the liberals' turn to feel the whip.

'*Doctor Zhivago* was published in the West three years ago,' Antaeus went on. 'At the time none of those guys even mentioned it. But now he's got the Nobel Prize they're obliged to take a stand.'

'By chance, I read a few pages of it,' I said.

'Really? How?'

'Part of a typescript I found in an empty apartment. But I didn't know what book it was.'

'Don't breathe a word of it to anybody. You could get into serious trouble over nothing.'

All around us the crowd of students was buzzing with talk.

'So what are they going to do with Pasternak now?' somebody asked.

'Who knows? Maybe he'll be deported.'

'What?'

'I said, maybe they'll send him away, rusticate him. Remember, Ovid was exiled to Romania . . .'

'Shut up, you idiot!'

'Do you think they really are capable of doing such a thing?' I asked Antaeus.

'I wouldn't be surprised.'

'To Romania,' somebody we couldn't see repeated. 'Like Ovid . . .'

'Apparently they're having talks right now. It's a peculiar argument . . . but I don't know the details.'

'Don't worry, I won't ask any questions!'

The whole trouble comes from Romania, I thought, collapsing with fatigue. It's no coincidence that the previous evening I had thought of Trajan's column. I could still feel the bruises on my skull from the hoofs of the Roman and Dacian horsemen. 'What about Vukmanović-Tempo? Has he left Moscow?' I asked.

'I've no idea,' Antaeus replied. 'Maybe he's still here.'

The bell rang for the last lecture and the courtyard

emptied. Only a few shreds remained of a newspaper that somebody must have used as wrapping. On the separate pieces you could see groups of capital letters spelling out RNAK, VAG, then ZHIV, STERN and PAST.

The campaign against Boris Pasternak had started twenty-four hours ago and was being conducted with great intensity throughout the Soviet Union. On the radio from five a.m. until midnight, on television, in newspapers and magazines and even in children's comics, the renegade writer was being spattered with venom. As was customary in cases of this kind, the bristling statements of Soviet literati were regurgitated by workers and collective farmers. Newspapers apologised for being able to publish only a minute proportion of the tens of thousands of letters and telegrams pouring in from the four corners of the Soviet lands. Among them were expressions of outrage from oil drillers, drama students, Orthodox priests, Bolshoi ballerinas, mountain climbers, atomic physicists, beekeepers, Caspian Sea salt-rakers, reformed mystics, the mute, and so forth. On the front page of *Literaturnaya gazeta* they'd printed statements by Shakenov and Ladonshchikov, among others. Most of the students on our course had also sent in statements and expected to see them in print in due course. One of them was Taburokov, who still believed that the Nobel Prize was awarded by the American government in cahoots with the Jewish lobby in New York. Another was Maskiavicius, even though he'd told me the previous day that Pasternak, despite his turpitude, was worth a hundred times more than any of the other runts of Soviet literature.

I had just come out of the last lecture when he told me there was a letter waiting for me in the porter's lodge. I recognised Lida's handwriting on the envelope. As I opened it I realised I had never before opened a letter with so much feeling. It had been mailed that same morning and it began without any preamble:

Since we met I've always liked you but I've never been completely in love with you. The day before yesterday I loved you, I couldn't say why. Perhaps love came through compassion. In Old Russian, the words for 'to love' and 'to sympathise' used to be the same, then they split apart. That evening you looked so distraught that it broke my heart. In my memory that evening is a nightmare. It hardly matters that we have broken up. I would just like you to remember me kindly. As for me, I will remember that night with horror and with compassion (love). Lida Snegina

PS All day yesterday the radio went on and on about a writer who committed betrayal and I thought of you. L.

I folded it rapidly and stuffed it into my pocket. I was beside myself, not because of the letter but at the thought of what I had done after Lida and I had parted. Ha! I thought. Now you're showing sympathy by delving into etymology and Church Slavonic. I was in a temper and it occurred to me that nobody could tell which of us was more to be pitied. Then, in a tangled skein, Stulpanc came to my mind, the way I'd handed Lida over to him as if we'd been at a slave market. In parallel, or like a substratum, I thought that it was all a diversion, an illusion of revenge and, looking at things in simple terms, mere nastiness on my part.

I was pacing up and down the courtyard like a madman, looking out for Stulpanc. I hadn't seen him since that crazy conversation. At one point I'd been tempted to call a halt to it and tell him the whole thing had been a joke, but then I remembered I had given him Lida's telephone number, which anchored it to reality. Two or three times I told myself that he had surely forgotten the episode, especially because he had been drunk at the time and had probably dropped the piece of paper with the phone number on it somewhere in the corridor. But each time I managed to reassure myself, doubts beset me again.

Suddenly I caught sight of him from behind, standing placidly at the Institute door, amid a group of students talking among themselves as they made for the trolleybus stop. I followed them at a distance of twenty yards or so. I just had to get into the same carriage as they did.

The trolleybus was half empty and I found a place near the rear window. Now and again I looked at Stulpanc's open, honest face from the corner of my eye. I was torn. Should I go up to him or not? I was vaguely afraid that my appearance would remind him of the accursed words we had spoken, and that perhaps he had not forgotten them entirely.

The trolleybus gradually filled. Now that I could no longer see Stulpanc I stopped torturing myself. I would not have been able to get to him now even if I'd wanted to.

At one point, I'm not sure how, I caught sight of his golden, perfectly brushed hair and, in a flash, I thought I'd done the right thing in handing Lida over to him, rather than to Abdullakhanov or the two Shotas. Then I told myself once more that the whole thing had been a bad joke he must have forgotten by now and that in a few days' time I would call Lida and we would make up as we had in the past.

Through the rear window I gazed at the street that led to Butyrsky Khutor, which looked more miserable than ever. Stulpanc got off with four or five others at the stop near to Novoslobodskaya metro station, which surprised me. I watched them cross the road and walk towards the great reddish walls of Butyrky Prison, and it came back to me: they were going to see one of their friends, someone called Kolya Krasnikov. He'd been sentenced to eight years in prison because some time earlier, when Tito was visiting Moscow, he'd shouted at a meeting, 'Long live the Tito-Ranković Clique!' They'd asked me to go with them, and as I was curious to see the inside of a Soviet prison, I nearly said yes. But then I remembered I was a foreigner, and also the police summons, so I said no.

The trolleybus was now packed. Squeezed up against the rear window, I uttered two or three of those little sighs that the sight of a street in winter sometimes arouses. I was dead tired.

At the front door of the residence stood a tall man, boyishly skinny with colourless hair and a cigarette stuck between his lips, like the ones you don't actually smoke. It was Zhenya Yevtushenko.

'Have you seen Bella?' he asked.

I shook my head, but it seemed obvious he didn't give a damn where Bella was.

'You seen that?' he questioned, directing his eyes to his right-hand jacket pocket from which a copy of *Literaturnaya gazeta* was poking out, showing half of Pasternak's name.

'Yes, I've read it,' I said.

'Hee-hee,' he said, with a triumphant grin. 'The Nobel . . . at last!'

You could see straight away that he, too, was one of the disappointed ghosts. He was about to say something more but just then Ira Emelianova passed us, a sad smile hovering in the corners of her eyes and on her lips, as if she was about to burst into tears. She greeted us nervously and Yevtushenko then asked me, 'You know who this Irochka is?'

I didn't understand his question.

In a whisper, he added, 'She's the daughter of Pasternak's mistress, a woman called Olga, who's been divorced three or four times, and is said to be the root of all the misfortunes that have befallen poor Boris Leonidovich.'

He went on talking about their relationship, but I had stopped listening. I'd had only a few hours of troubled sleep over the last two nights, and I was exhausted. By the time I got to the door of my room I was in that strange state when you're on the verge of sleep – I could feel dreams rising from my limbs, soft and porous, like sponges, and I felt I had only to stretch out my hand to touch or seize them or push them a little further away. I was sufficiently awake to realise that the spongy sensation beneath my belt belonged to the world of dream, and sufficiently asleep to feel it was completely natural, to the point that I was unable to escape from it. In my dreams I was lying in a large bath, and although the art history professor, whose job it was to turn on the hot tap, kept saying, '*Ubr jazëk*,' the water still would not come. Then she declared, 'We are in the very hammam where Aragon, Elsa Triolet and Lida took a bath, but the aesthetico-ideological nature of a hammam is conditioned in the first place by *tuuli unch bll*, that is to say by the typical situation . . . in other words by *tuuli zox* . . .'

When I woke, night had fallen almost completely. I stretched out my arm mechanically and switched on the radio. The anti-Pasternak campaign continued. I listened for a while with my hands behind my head. After a feature on a women's meeting in Irkutsk, they read a statement from Anatoly Kuznetsov. It was the harshest of all those I had heard. My room was now almost totally dark. A few shards of light that had been trapped in the curtains wavered gently over my head. And it's not even evening yet! I thought. Darkness suited evenings and night, but when it came before the end of the day it depressed me more than anything. I was alone, in the midst of an afternoon that might just as well have been called an after-midnight, with a radio blaring ceaselessly over a landmass of twenty-two million square kilometres. 'One sixth of the earth drowning in such insults!' I muttered to myself drowsily.

Then, all of a sudden, I shuddered. My mind now sharpened like a steel dagger, I took the full measure of the infernal machine running full speed ahead. What must it be like to be the target, to be the eye of that whirlwind?

I imagined the legendary Slav head puffing out its cheeks in the middle of the steppe. Soviet propaganda was just like it. A few years earlier that head had raised a dust-storm against Stalin, and now, who knew why, it was blowing against its own supporters. What must it be like to be the target of all these attacks? I wondered again. I switched on my bedside lamp. How had it all been set in motion? I had no idea – I couldn't imagine how it had been achieved. I knew of not a single work of Soviet literature that gave even a fragmentary description of how the machinery of state actually functioned: no insight into meetings of the Council of Ministers of the USSR, or the Politburo, or other more occult authorities. Antaeus and I had talked about it once at the Praga café. He hadn't come across any either.

But – I thought in my puzzlement – maybe I'm wrong, maybe such works do exist and I just haven't had an opportunity to read them yet. I recalled that last week Shogentsukov had given me a signed copy of one of his works that had been translated and published in Moscow. Where had I put it? I got up, in a daze, and found it only after I'd emptied all the drawers in my desk. The radio didn't stop bawling. Shogentsukov, a former prime minister, must surely deal with the problems of the state somewhere or other. Yes, he must! I sat on the edge of my bed and, despite the migraine that was tormenting me, I started to read. The radio suspended its rant and broadcast some music, but even those sounds felt charged with hatred. After thirty minutes I cast the book aside. It was a novella-length idyll among shepherds, pastures and hills. Not only did it contain no mention

of the institutions of the state, it did not admit of a single
construction in brick or stone. Nothing but gurgling streams,
fidelity and flowers, and a few hymns sung of an evening
to the glory of the Communist Party of the USSR. Can
this really be? I wondered.

On the radio the anti-Pasternak diatribe had resumed.
The announcer read out a letter from the people of a region
of Qipstap, on the steppe, then a statement by the Tashkent
clergy. A sixth of the globe was awash once more under a
tidal wave of invective. In recent times so many important
events had taken place – there had been so many tragic
reversals: whole central committees had been thrown out,
factions had fought implacably to gain or retain power,
there'd been plots and backstage deals. But none of that,
or almost none, showed up on the pages of novels or in
the speeches of characters on stage. All you got was the
rustling of birch trees – ah! my beloved silver birch! – and
in all that literature it was always Sunday, as it had been on
the day we were skiing at Peredelkino.

I got up, dressed and went into the corridor. I was at a
loose end and just sauntered up and down. The dim bulbs
gave off a wan light and now and again you could hear
the lift humming. I knocked at Stulpanc's door a couple of
times but there was no answer. Where have they all gone?
I wondered. I went back to my room and stood in front
of the radio with my arms at my sides, almost standing to
attention, as if I'd just heard a sentence handed down by a
court. The campaign was still going on. Some statement
was being made in elaborately convoluted prose, maybe by
the North Sea whaling fleet. Not much later I was in the

corridor again, and as I wandered up and down, I found myself in front of Stulpanc's door more than once. Where has he gone? an inner voice asked. It was buried deep inside me, but I could feel it rising to the surface. As my hand reached out mechanically to knock on Stulpanc's door for the fourth time I realised that I had been waiting in the corridor for his return. In my muddled mind I tried to imagine where he had gone to hide, but it took me a while to convince myself that it was a useless game, and that it mattered not a jot to me whether Stulpanc was at the bar of the *Kavkaz*, the editorial offices of *Tabak*, having lunch with Khrushchev or supping with the Devil himself. The only thing that mattered was that he was not with one particular person – Lida. I couldn't believe he'd have phoned her so soon and it was even less believable that he'd got a date already. That's impossible, I said to myself. Stulpanc is a plodder in that department. And then, if she'd written me such a sorrowful letter, it wasn't so she could fall into someone else's arms!

But one minute later I was convinced the opposite was the case. It wasn't possible that Stulpanc had refrained from trying to get in touch with such a pretty woman. He'd seemed entranced by her. No, no, there was no reason for him to have put off calling her. As for Lida, her letter, the feelings she'd put into it, the Old Russian and all that, wouldn't have prevented her running off with Stulpanc – quite the opposite, if all she'd written to me was true and if therefore her affection for me, the etymology, the Old Russian and all that such things entailed, had reached the state she had claimed, then of course, once she'd heard about the disaster (because that idiot Stulpanc must surely have told her I was dead), she must have dropped everything to hurry round to see him to find out more. Yes! Yes! I almost cried aloud in despair. He called her and she's gone out with him on a date! Especially because, on this ice-cold day, all she had to listen to was this unending campaign, which must have made her think about writers and similarly sinister matters. I shouldn't have let Stulpanc out of my sight on a day like this.

I was at my wit's end. I'd spent half an hour shuttling back and forth between my room and the corridor, so I decided to go out to cool off.

A chilly breeze was whirling snowflakes into spirals under the lamp posts. I got onto a trolleybus that took me to Pushkin Square. Gorky Street looked quite beautiful in the snow. I walked to the Artists' Café where I'd decided to have dinner. To hell with the pair of them! I thought, in a sudden burst of indifference. The snow, the wind and the street in its winter attire had clarified my feelings. It all seemed simpler now. They were in their own country, they could get married and have children, whereas I was only in transit. *In transit* seemed a good way to refer to myself in the soggy, soporific season of winter that I had lived through up to this point. *In transit,* I repeated to myself, and the Russian word *vremmeny* – 'provisional' – merged in my mind with the name of Vukmanović-Tempo. Yes, to hell with them! I ordered a glass of wine, and a little later I came out of the restaurant and went back to the bus stop in a thoroughly good mood.

*

The first thing that struck me when I reached the residence was the light streaming from under Stulpanc's door. I felt a pang in my heart. I no longer had the support of snow-covered open spaces and I almost fainted. I hurried on and pushed into his room without knocking. He was smoking a cigarette. I tried not to speak too quickly.

'So where did you get to, then?'

Guilt and surprise were combined in the smile that spread across his broad Nordic face. I'd never burst into his room before with a plaintive 'So where did you get to?'

'Well?' I added.

'What?'

'Where were you?'

He stared at me with pale eyes that seemed not to have enough room in his face. At last he replied, 'Well, I was out, with her.'

'With Lida?'

He nodded, without ceasing to stare at me.

Gently, in heavy silence, something broke inside me. So there you are, I said to myself. I felt a great emptiness. Ideas and words had simply flown. All that was left were a few scraps of language, sounds like *um* and *I see* and *really*. I remembered that whenever I had had an upset of this kind, words had left me just as plant life deserts areas where the climate is too harsh; all I had left were clipped syllables of that sort, as if only they could tolerate the sudden worsening of the climate inside me.

'But you yourself said . . .' Stulpanc began. He surely meant to say, 'You palmed her off on me,' but apparently he found it too direct, or too vulgar, to say outright.

My mind was a blank and I studied a picture on the wall. It depicted a sight I knew: Sigurd's castle in Latvia. I'd visited it the previous summer.

'But didn't you set me up?'

'Yes, yes, of course.'

'I can see you've had a change of heart. But if you like . . .'

'What?' My voice had gone faint despite all my efforts to make it sound normal.

'If you like . . . though now, of course, the case is closed. Yes! To hell with it!'

I'd lost the thread. Who or what was supposed to go to hell? Could nothing be salvaged? 'Did you tell her I was dead?'

He swallowed, then admitted it. 'In a manner of speaking, yes.'

'I'd hoped you would be kinder!' Now I knew the truth, words had returned to me. 'Yes, kinder!' I repeated, doing my best to laugh as I said it. 'It's just like you to pass a death sentence on me!'

'But you asked me to say that! And you went so far as to tell me I should say you had died in a plane crash. Don't you remember?'

'That really takes the biscuit! I was drunk, for heaven's sake! Didn't you notice?'

'Do you think I was sober?'

I thought, It's all over now. Now she believes I am dead, it's all done for. 'If only you hadn't killed me off entirely,' I said, with a flicker of optimism. Just before, when I'd asked him if he'd told Lida of my death, he'd replied, 'In a manner of speaking . . .' 'You could have told her I was only injured . . .'

Now Stulpanc lost his temper. 'You need your head examining!' he shouted. 'You got me into this. I've never played that sort of trick. You've turned me into a kind of Chichikov from *Dead Souls*. I'd never have called the girl if she hadn't attracted me so . . . so . . . What's the Russian adverb to express an absolute superlative?'

'Insanely.'

'That's right! Attracted me so insanely!'

We stood there without speaking for a few seconds. I examined the Latvian castle on the wall, trying to summon up some memory of the previous summer I'd spent in Stulpanc's country, but it was now light years away.

'All right, all right,' I said wearily. 'How did she take it?'

He saw that I had calmed down and smiled faintly, without looking at me. 'She was very upset . . .' He was staring at the floor, but I kept my eyes on him. 'Yes, she was very, very upset,' he repeated. 'Insanely so.' I thought, To be pitied by someone, to arouse sympathy in Old Russian . . . 'She even wept. Yes, she cried a couple of times. I saw tears in her eyes . . .'

I sighed deeply, trying not to make a sound to prevent Stulpanc noticing I had sighed. I felt strangely relieved. Maybe things were better like this. If they'd been different, perhaps she would never have had a chance to cry over me. Suddenly a vague, lukewarm feeling spread through my chest. My ribs began to soften and bend as if they were in a surrealist painting. One day you will cry over me . . . Two days earlier such a thought would have made me laugh out loud. Ah! She's crying! Little Lida is upset! Tut-tut! I was making superhuman efforts to hold down a great guffaw accompanied by those clucking noises I found so repellent in other people, but I failed. But far from succeeding in clucking, like the ne'er-do-wells of Gorky Street, I couldn't even manage to laugh naturally, like an ordinary person. The whole thing seemed more and more primitive to me. I must have been waiting years for someone to shed tears on my behalf. I'd longed for tears with a more terrible thirst than a parched Bedouin in the deserts of Arabia. Over the last two years I'd had relationships with young women who were very free: I'd taken them to the theatre, to cafés, on night trains; we'd danced and kissed and slept together without ever saying, 'I love you', because it seemed old-fashioned, and recently we'd gone so far as to replace the word *lyublyu* ('I love') with the word *seksyu*, and were very proud of our invention. So we'd said a lot of stupid things and done just as many, following our whims from bars to dance halls, and from there, blindly and joyfully, onto a snowy downhill slope. This long pilgrimage through the desert, in gradual stages, without my noticing, but to an unbearable degree, had given me that thirst for a few tears. At last they had been shed. It had taken the intercession of death to bring those tiny blue drops into being.

'What a peculiar fellow you are,' Stulpanc said.

So that was it! She liked dead men more than the living. And his words of consolation had not been wasted.

'You really are funny,' Stulpanc went on. 'At first, when you came in, you looked like a thundercloud, but now you're almost smiling. Did you know that sudden changes of mood are supposed to be one of the first symptoms of madness?'

I went on staring him in the eye. 'Yes,' I agreed. 'It's quite possible I'm going off my rocker, seeing what I did.'

The following morning was as gloomy as the ones that preceded it. I'd barely washed when I switched on the radio, automatically. The campaign hadn't stopped. The diatribes were the same as before but they were now being spoken in a graver tone. You could sense straight away that a new phase of the campaign was being launched that day. There was no doubt that it had been worked out in advance in great detail. The gigantic state propaganda machine never slumbered.

There was an unusual bustle at the Gorky Institute. The consequences of Sunday's drinking – puffy cheeks, blotches, bags under the eyes – had been finally wiped from faces that henceforth expressed only sinister harshness.

After the second period, posters appeared on the walls of all corridors announcing an ultra-important meeting that afternoon. It was rumoured that the most eminent writers of the Soviet Union would attend, and there was even talk that the presidents of the Writers' Unions of the People's Republics had been called to Moscow and would probably be there.

Meanwhile the Institute's inmates carried on sending statements to the papers and to radio and television stations. Taburokov alone had sent pieces to fourteen different reviews and newspapers; in one he'd even described Pasternak as an enemy of the Arab nation. On the second day of the campaign one hundred and eleven dailies and seventy-four periodicals had published editorials, articles, statements and reports condemning Pasternak. More such pieces were expected in other daily, weekly and fortnightly publications and then in monthly and bi-monthly journals, science magazines, quarterlies, bilingual reviews and so on.

'He ought to make a statement this evening turning down the Nobel,' Maskiavicius said. 'If it's not wrapped up by eight tonight, the campaign will get even nastier.'

'How could it be nastier than it is?' someone asked.

'Apparently,' Maskiavicius answered, 'the patriarch of Soviet letters, Korney Chukovsky, is going to call on him at two this afternoon to try to persuade him.'

'And if he fails?'

'Then we'll have a big meeting.'

'To what purpose?'

'I suspect we'll move to menace, third degree.'

'Where did you learn all that?'

'I know what I know,' said Maskiavicius. 'That's all.'

'But what if he doesn't turn down the prize even after the third degree? What happens then? Will there be a fourth degree?'

Maskiavicius interrupted the speaker. 'You won't catch me out as easily as that, mate! I wouldn't be so careless as to tell you anything about the fourth degree. Sss.' He whistled. 'Fourth degree! Hey-hey! Degree number four . . . Hm! Brrr!' With a diabolical glint in his eye, he turned tail and disappeared into the crowd.

The meeting was held in the auditorium on the first floor of the Institute. Almost all the seats were taken when I went in. It was already twilight outside and the feeble light that trickled through the tall bay windows seemed to form an alloy with the bronze chandeliers that hadn't yet been switched on, though I didn't know why. The room was packed and virtually silent. The scraping of a chair and words whispered into neighbours' ears could not dent the empire of silence. On the contrary: the occasional sounds of creaking seats and muffled gossip made the atmosphere only more leaden.

I was standing at the entrance, unsure what to do, when I noticed people waving at me. It was the two Shotas, Maskiavicius and Kurganov, who were almost sitting in each other's laps. I forged a path between the rows of seats, and my fellow students huddled even closer together to make just enough room for me. In the row in front of us were the Karakums and somewhere to the side I thought I could see one of the 'Belarusian Virgins'.

'How are you?' someone asked me quietly.

I shrugged. The mood was such that you didn't have the slightest wish to answer anything about yourself. In that drab room you felt as though you could speak only about generalities, and only through the use of impersonal verbs, if possible in a chorus, as in some ancient drama.

I looked around at the participants. Apart from the students and teachers of the Institute, there were many known faces. The front rows were almost completely filled with literary mediocrities. They were just as I had always seen them, always present and totally invulnerable, sitting shoulder to shoulder in the front rank, stepping up to glorify Stalin before anyone else, and to drop him in favour of

Khrushchev; they were quite capable of deserting Khrushchev for some other First Secretary.

Right at the back, in a corner, in the middle of a group that remained obscure, I thought I could make out Paustovsky. Was it a group of the silent opposition or of Jewish writers? I couldn't see them clearly enough. It was getting ever darker in the room. At long last someone thought of switching on the lights. The candelabra immediately banished the weak daylight and filled the hall with a light that reminded me of Ladonshchikov – a brightness tainted with anxiety. The first thing the light revealed was the long table of the Presidium, decked out in red velvet. The porcelain vases at each end and the bouquet in the middle made it look like an elongated catafalque. I recalled the wallpaper on the walls of the empty apartment where I had read a few pages of *Doctor Zhivago*. It was no coincidence that its pattern had made me think of the lid of a sarcophagus.

'What does the third degree consist of?' I asked in a whisper. 'Is that what we're about to see?'

'I don't know. Maybe we will, maybe we won't. It depends on Chukovsky, who's gaga already.'

'I meant to ask, what exactly has he done?'

'Nothing, apparently. Around two he went to Pasternak's *dacha* at Peredelkino, but it seems he forgot why he was there. So he drank a cup of tea, and then had a nap on the sofa.'

I was just about to guffaw, but at that moment a kind of shiver ran through the room. The meeting's Presidium had come on to the stage to take their seats at the long table with its crimson drapery. The first were already sitting down while others, who were still in the audience, were lining up and creeping forward in waves, like a snake. Their whispered names circulated among us. They'd been summoned from here and there; most were old, some had been publishing trilogies for forty years; if my memory serves me right, five had published novels with titles that contained the word 'earth', and two had gone blind. My mind went back to Korney Chukovksy's fateful siesta, but I couldn't manage to laugh about it.

'Comrades, we are gathered here today . . .'

The opening speaker was Seriogin, director of the Gorky Institute. His eyes, as always, had a sinister and malicious glint. To his right sat Druzin, representing the governing body of the Writers' Union. His hair was snow white, but his massive head and thrusting jaw seemed so fierce and warlike that it was hard to believe the white hair was real.

'We are gathered here to censure, to . . .'

Seriogin's voice contained the same proportion of malice and gall as his eyes, the stripes on his suit and even his hands, one of which had been replaced by a black rubber prosthesis. The first time I saw him I supposed he'd lost his hand in the war, but Maskiavicius told me that Seriogin's hand had slowly withered of its own accord in the course of the third Five-year Plan . . .

Seriogin's speech was a short one. Then Druzin rose. His contribution was no more drawn out; what he said didn't match his white hair. As always, everything about him jutted like his chin.

'Now for the fireworks!' Maskiavicius said, once Druzin had sat down.

Indeed, at that point dozens of hands were raised to request the floor. From the outset it was clear that, as was customary in such circumstances, the Presidium's selection of speakers sought to maintain some kind of balance between generations, nationalities and regions, as well as between undeclared literary groupings.

Ladonshchikov was among the first allowed to speak. In a special voice that was both gloomy and booming (a Party voice, in Maskiavicius's phrase), in a voice that his lungs could only ever produce on occasions of this kind, Ladonshchikov made the proposal to his silent listeners that Pasternak be expelled from the Soviet Union.

'Was that the third degree?' I whispered in Maskiavicius's ear.

He nodded.

'If he fails to make a decision by eight p.m. . . .'

All those who spoke after Ladonshchikov supported the proposal, without exception.

It was one of the Shotas' turn when I realised I hadn't seen Stulpanc. All around the hall dozens of hands were still being raised.

'Have you seen Stulpanc?' I asked Maskiavicius.

'No,' he answered. 'That's a point. What's he up to?'

One of the 'Belarusian Virgins' has just walked on to the stage.

I hadn't seen Antaeus either.

'Now it's the Karakums' turn,' said Maskiavicius. 'That should be a laugh!'

It was as clear as daylight: Stulpanc was with Lida Snegina while this was going on . . .

Now it was Taburokov's turn.

I told myself that I had never had occasion to wile away a campaign of denunciation in the company of a young woman . . .

Taburokov must have said something peculiar because the audience was trying to stifle a groan.

Being alone with a girl, I thought, in the course of a campaign or something of that sort, such as an epidemic – now that would most likely stick in your memory for a good long while . . .

After a couple of first-year women had said their piece, Yuri Goncharov and Abdullakhanov took their turn. Then Anatoly Kuznetsov was called to the podium.

I thought I glimpsed Ira Emelianova's blonde hair behind Paustovsky. He had Yuri Pankratov and Vania Kharabarov to each side. One was tall and thin and moved his arms stiffly, like a robot; the other was short and looked repulsive.

'I'm looking at them as well,' Maskiavicius said, in my ear. 'You know they're both spies for Pasternak? They're here to pick up everything that's said about him and then they'll report back to him.'

'Ah!' I said, lost for words.

'Is Yevtushenko going to speak?' someone asked, from the row behind me.

Where Yevtushenko was concerned, I'd heard people utter every imaginable insult and every imaginable compliment about him.

At this point a member of the panel shouted, 'Maskiavicius, you have the floor!'

He glanced at me, then stood up and made his way to the podium.

'As long as we are together, what does it matter if the world is going to ruin . . .' I recited the two lines from De Rada automatically in my head. In his novel the lovers meet during an earthquake.

On the stage, speakers came and went. Then a muffled mumble swept through the hall. Pasternak was racing across the tundra: Kyuzengesh was about to hold forth!

Stulpanc and Lida were perhaps listening to it all on the radio, in the corner of some café. They were gazing into each other's eyes and maybe they were talking about me.

Amplified to a terrifying degree by the loudspeakers, Kyuzengesh's murmuring now filled the whole hall.

Yes, they must have occasion to talk about me. Did she not like dead writers? Once again we had mounted the same horse: I was the dead and she was the living rider, like the legendary Kostandin and Doruntine. Except that instead of there being two, there were now three of us: the living couple, and the deceased me.

The campaign went on. Nothing was known for certain about the outcome of the Gorky Institute meeting as far as Pasternak's expulsion from the Soviet Union was concerned. Some people said he had already sent an urgent telegram to Stockholm to decline the prize, others that he was still wavering. In the best-informed circles, they were saying he'd written a moving letter to Khrushchev and that his fate now hung on the First Secretary's response. But they were also claiming that Khrushchev had been furious with writers for some time, and only a very harsh reply could be expected.

Meanwhile gusts of icy wind bore down on Moscow. Sometimes you could hear them howling as they blew in from some indeterminate point. At Butyrsky Khutor it seemed as if they were coming from Ostankino, but in that corner of town people reckoned they'd been let loose in the centre, near the main squares.

All through the long moan of winter Stulpanc went on seeing Lida. They sometimes talked about me, he said. It sounded macabre. Breaking all the laws of death, he informed me about how mine had occurred. It was against nature for anybody to hear about that, because nobody can ever know such things. But there did exist in this world one being for whom I counted as dead, and so, objectively speaking, some part of me must have passed to the hereafter. And that being, Lida Snegina, was the only person in whom the details of my death were located. Lida was my pyramid and my mausoleum; she was where my sarcophagus lay. Through her, the whole relationship between my being and my nothingness had been turned upside down. And when Stulpanc came back from spending time with her, I felt as if he was returning from the other world, coming down from a higher plane, from an alternative time with newspapers bearing future dates and archives containing information about me that looked like nothing at all, since no one had yet looked at me in the light of my own death.

Sometimes it seemed to me that my death was also being broadcast through Stulpanc's eyes. On a couple of occasions when he'd looked as if he wanted to talk to me, I'd cut him off: 'Say no more!'

At one of the anti-Pasternak meetings I'd made the acquaintance of Alla Grachova, a theatre-loving girl with a sense of humour. Every time the radio announcers returned to the subject of Pasternak after a musical broadcast, she would take my hand and say, 'Let's go somewhere else!'

But the campaign was all around us and nobody could get free of it. It had winkled its way inside us. When Alla talked about some of her relatives, she told me what they were saying about Pasternak. One of her uncles was the angriest of them all.

'But you told me he'd made his career since the rise of Khrushchev!'

'Yes, he's a Khrushchevite through and through, and a dyed-in-the-wool anti-Stalinist too.'

'But how can that be possible?'

She looked at me sweetly, as if she didn't understand what wasn't possible. I decided to explain it to her in simple terms.

'Your uncle paints Pasternak as black as coal, right?' She nodded. 'And he also heaps insults on Stalin, right?'

'Yes,' said Alla, eyes wide.

'And Pasternak most certainly slings mud at Stalin. In other words, your uncle has the same attitude to Stalin as Pasternak does. Right? Well, then, arithmetically, between your uncle and Pasternak there should not be any incompatibility. Quite the opposite, actually.'

'Damn!' she said. 'I can never get the hang of that kind

TWILIGHT OF THE EASTERN GODS

of thing and I've no wish to. We'd said we'd drop the subject. You can't imagine the goings-on at our place . . .'

All the same, newspapers, radio and TV carried on campaigning. *Doctor . . . Doctor . . .* The wailing of the transcontinental wind made it seem as if the entire, and now almost entirely snow-covered, Soviet Union was calling out for a man in a white coat. *Doctor . . . Doctor . . .* Sometimes, at dusk or in the half-light of dawn, you could almost hear the deep-throated moaning of an invalid waiting for the arrival from who knew where of a doctor who had so far failed to turn up.

The campaign stopped as suddenly as it had started. One fine morning the radio began broadcasting reports on the achievements of the collective farms in the Urals, about summer retreats, about arts festivals in one or another Soviet republic, about the abundance of the fisheries, about contented young people in the steppe near the Volga – but it uttered not another word about Pasternak.

It was the same in the papers and on TV, in the streets, on the bus and in the corridors of the Institute. Twelve hours earlier the name of Pasternak had come out of people's mouths with an angry, violent snarl; now it didn't seem anyone could even get it out properly any more.

'What's going on?' I asked Antaeus. 'Could this be the fourth degree that Maskiavicius mentioned?'

'Hard to tell. Apparently, it wasn't needed.'

'What do you mean? Why did there have to be exactly that much, neither more nor less? Can you tell me that? Speak, O Greek!'

· 141 ·

In the corridor, in the cloakroom, on the staircase, out in the courtyard – not a word. I was tempted to go and question Maskiavicius in person: could this be the fourth degree? But I thought better of it. Everybody was converging on the auditorium where, as if to rub out the memory of the sinister anti-Pasternak event, there'd just been an enthusiastic reception for a friend of the Soviet Union, the Malagasy poetess Andriamampandri Ratsifandrihamanana, to be followed shortly by an equally warm-spirited reception for the eminent leader of the Algerian Communist Party, Larbi Bouhali.

Today was different in every way from the cloudy Pasternakian yesterday. The walls were plastered with posters bearing exclamatory slogans praising Soviet-Algerian friendship. The drapery that covered the long table of the Presidium had acquired a purplish hue. Red canvas banners bore slogans where *USSR* and *Algeria* were accompanied by words like 'heroic', 'blood', 'freedom', 'bombs' and 'flag'. Over the loudspeaker came revolutionary marching songs.

At last he made his entrance to a long ovation, waving at the audience, smiling and cheerful: a positive hero emerging without transition from the fire of epic combat. The clapping didn't stop all the time he was walking slowly towards the podium. Just as Larbi Bouhali got to the steps that led up to the lectern, Seriogin and a colleague took hold of him by the arms, and that was when the whole audience, through the mist of strong emotion, realised that he had a gammy leg, or perhaps an artificial one. That was all it took for the ovation to rise to a new level (level four), in a paroxysm that had to end in screaming. Eyes were watering, and breathing felt like swallowing your neighbour's exhalation. Seriogin gestured to the audience in a way that suggested, 'That's enough . . . such strong feelings . . . at your age . . .' In the row behind mine, Shakenov had already launched into one of his heroic ballads and the 'Belarusian Virgins' had taken out their handkerchiefs, while Antaeus hissed something hateful into my left ear. He sounded as if he was speaking from far away. 'It's all a lie, believe me. I know the story well. He hasn't set foot in Algeria for years. As for his leg, he broke it when he was skiing some-where on the outskirts of Moscow. You got that? He broke his leg skiing. That scoundrel has a *dacha* next door to a Greek guy, who told me about it. Sure, he's an imposter, you understand? A fraud!'

When the meeting was over Antaeus and I left together. I hadn't seen Stulpanc anywhere.

'Some militant that was!' Antaeus muttered, from time to time. We were both in the darkest of moods. In Algeria there was bloody carnage, and that bastard was waiting for the war to end so he could return and seize power. 'And then he'll sell his country to the Soviet Union for a *dacha* and a pair of slippers! Oh! I'm going to burst!'

I'd never seen Antaeus so indignant. As he spoke his face twisted as if his war wounds were hurting him again. Maybe they were.

'Are the plans for the meeting going ahead?' I asked, to change the subject.

'What meeting?'

It was some time before he grasped which meeting I was talking about.

'Oh, I see,' he said eventually. 'Yes, sure, the subcommittees are hard at work . . .'

The subcommittees are hard at work . . . I repeated to myself. O Ancient Athenian, tell me, why does that send a shiver down my spine?

We parted at the Novoslobodskaya metro station. I decided to walk all the way back to Butyrsky Khutor. It was a grey day; the buildings went on and on in interminable and depressingly monotonous rows, and the hundreds of windows, perhaps because of their skimpy panes, had a malicious look about them. I crossed Sushchevsky Val, but it was still a long way to the residence. The hundreds of television antennae on the roofs of the houses looked like so many walking-sticks raised in anger by a crowd of old folk. Four days previously, Pasternak's name had been pouring down on them, like black snow. I went on past Saviolovsky Voksal, cursing myself for not having caught a bus. An old house had been knocked down and bulldozers were shovelling away the rubble.

What a stressful week! I thought, staring at a half-demolished concrete pillar with wire reinforcements sticking out at the top, like uncombed hair. I walked on a bit and then – who knows why? – turned round to contemplate that lump of concrete: a pillar that had lost its head.

The week ended with the death of the famous story-teller Akulina. Although she was illiterate she had long been granted membership of the Soviet Writers' Union, and the entire complement of the Gorky Institute attended her funeral at the Novodevichy Cemetery.

A sharp wind swayed the leafless branches of the trees. It seemed to hiss the traditional opening of a Russian folktale: once upon a time, in some kingdom, in some state . . . в неком царстве, в неком государстве . . .

For half an hour we processed behind the pink-silk-draped coffin of the old lady who had told so many stories about the creatures of Slav myths, Scythian divinities and maybe also about that solitary head puffing out its cheeks to blow the wind across the steppe . . .

Once upon a time . . . жил-ъыл . . . No work of any period could have a more universal opening than that formula in the imperfect tense: once upon a time, there used to be . . . Nobody, no human generation, could ever do without it . . .

Once upon a time there used to be a foreigner who met a young Russian woman called Lida Snegina . . .

The long procession of mourners finally came to a standstill. Stulpanc had still not shown his face. Was he so much in love? Around marble tombs, bronze crosses and bare branches, the wind went on whistling the opening lines of fairy-tales. Once upon a time . . . жил-ъыл . . . The phrase seemed to come straight from the ancient lungs of the terrestrial globe . . . Once upon a time there used to be a giant state whose name was Soviet Union . . .

CHAPTER FIVE

A Muscovite artist had just flown back from India, bringing smallpox into the city. He'd caught it at the funeral of a princess in Delhi – imprudently, he had gone too close to the coffin to make a hasty sketch of some of the detail. He died a few days after landing in Moscow; his friends and relatives were expected to end in the same way.

Early one morning, in front of the porter's lodge at the Institute, a large poster went up, ordering the entire population of the city to be vaccinated, with a list of all the vaccination centres that had been set up. Anyone not following the order within forty-eight hours risked being quarantined.

A knot of people was looking at the poster.

'Serves us right,' Kurganov muttered. 'We've got far too cosy with India.'

'Did the epidemic come from there?' someone asked.

'Where else? You don't think it came from West Germany, do you?'

'That's enough, Kolya,' said his companion, tugging at his sleeve. 'Time to go and get that vaccination.'

'Kurganov's right,' said Maskiavicius, who had suddenly turned up. 'We really did get too close to the Indies and

Brahmaputras!' Someone else guffawed. 'Yes, that's how it goes. We make up with some people, and pick a fight with others.'

He gave me a sidelong glance, but I didn't respond. I'd turned to stone as I stood there reading the chilling words on the poster for maybe the tenth time. Inside, I felt something empty taking shape and a contraction somewhere near my diaphragm. It wasn't the first time I'd heard allusions of that kind in the last few days, but never had I heard one as clear as that.

I was walking down the street in a crowd of people, many of whom were on their way to the vaccination centres, when I caught sight of Maskiavicius again. I put on speed to catch up with him.

'Maskiavicius,' I said, taking his elbow. 'Listen to me. Just now beside the poster you said something, and I thought you meant it for me – or, rather, for my country. If you've heard anything, as a good comrade . . . if you're aware of what's going on . . . I beg you to let me know.'

He turned to me. 'I don't know anything,' he said, then hastened to add, 'I was joking.'

'No, that wasn't a joke. You're at liberty to say nothing, but you were not joking.'

'Yes, I was! It was a joke!' he said emphatically.

We walked on for a while without saying anything.

'Well, excuse me, then,' I said, and walked on faster to put some distance between us.

A few seconds later I smelt his breath over my right shoulder.

'Wait a moment! You think we're in every loop, that we're plotting against you because you're on your own and a foreigner, not to mention a heap of other reasons.' After a pause he added, with more feeling, 'That is what you think, isn't it?'

It was indeed the case, but as I was offended I didn't bother to turn my head to reply to him.

'Listen,' he went on, in the same tone, 'you know I'm not like Yuri Goncharov or Ladonshchikov or the fucking Virgins or other such scum of the earth. And you know full well that I'm not particularly fond of Russians. If I knew anything, I'd tell you straight away. I swear I know nothing precise. However . . . we were at the Aragvy restaurant the other day when a fellow who was there, and who isn't a friend of yours, said, 'The soup is hot, but things are cooling down between us and the Albanians.' I tried more than once to get him to talk but he wouldn't say anything else. So now do you believe me?'

I said nothing. I wasn't listening to him. I was just saying over and over to myself, Can this be true?

'And then, to be honest,' Maskiavicius went on, leaning on my shoulder, 'it would be a real stroke of luck if things were to go cold between us and you. Yes, I know, I'm Lithuanian, but don't make me say any more . . .'

Suddenly I felt it was all true. On that cold morning, among the flood of pedestrians hurrying to get themselves vaccinated against the dreadful sickness that the funeral of an Indian princess had brought to Moscow, it seemed that all the mist that had shrouded Antaeus's words about Vukmanović-Tempo coming to Moscow, about Bucharest or the planning subcommittees for the Moscow conference had lifted in a trice.

I could see my breath turning to haze as it left my mouth and I wouldn't have been surprised to see it fall to the ground and shatter into a thousand pieces of crystal. I was neither happy nor sad. I had resumed my state of chronic instability, beyond sadness and gaiety, in this glaucous universe, with its slanted, harsh and twisted light. Relations between my limbs had broken off. All the parts of my body were about to disconnect and reassemble themselves of their own free will in the most unbelievable ways: I might suddenly find I had an eye between my ribs, maybe even both eyes, or my legs attached to my arms, perhaps to make me fly.

As with all things beyond understanding, this metamorphosis possessed a mysterious beauty. A world sensation! Newspaper headlines. General stupefaction. The horror and grandeur of breaking off. I was spread out among them, as if I'd been scattered by a gale. A continuous burning tightness afflicted my throat. Then, as in a dream of flying, I thought I could see the black earth laid out beneath me, with a few chrome-ore freight wagons of the kind I used to notice in the goods station at Durrës on Sundays when I went to the beach with friends, alongside the barrels of bitumen that would sometimes be there when there'd been a hold-up in loading the ships, stacked in terrifying funereal mounds.

None of that did much to calm me, though I maintained an outward icy demeanour. The events of 1956 in Hungary. The Party Conference in Tirana that had taken place then, too, at which, for the first time, the Soviets had been spoken of unkindly . . .

'Now pull yourself together!' Maskiavicius said.

We would have to put up with economic sanctions, maybe a blockade or something worse. The legendary Slavic head would puff out his cheeks to raise a truly hellish wind that would blow all the way to Albania.

'I shouldn't have told you,' Maskiavicius mumbled, standing beside me.

The dreadful round face that seemed to have been born from the steppe merged in my mind with Khrushchev's.

'Name, first name, and date of birth,' a nurse said.

I was standing in front of a table laden with vials and lancets. All around, a constant hubbub of people coming and going. Maskiavicius had vanished.

'Take off your coat and jacket, please,' said the nurse. 'Roll up your shirt sleeve as far as you can.'

Out of the corner of my eye I watched her white fingers rub my upper arm with a cotton swab dipped in medicinal alcohol. Then they gripped a blood lancet and proceeded to make pricks in my skin with as much care as if they were tracing out an ancient pattern.

It occurred to me that the princess's coffin must have been decorated with really strange designs to have cast such a spell on the painter.

At the site of the butchery I saw blood about to spurt. Then the young woman's slender fingers placed a patch of damp gauze over the pattern.

'Don't roll down your sleeve until the bandage is dry,' she said.

★

On my way back to the Institute I couldn't stop turning over in my mind the brief conversation I'd had with Maskiavicius. Posters advising the people of Moscow to get vaccinated were plastered everywhere. Passers-by gathered in groups to read them line by line, nodding or chatting with each other. I stopped a few times at such gatherings in the absurd hope that someone would mention the particularly sunny relations with India and consequently the cooling of friendship with . . . with a certain country.

Antaeus wasn't at the residence. Apart from him, I didn't know anyone I could quiz openly on the subject so I put my overcoat back on and went out again. It was cold. With my mind a blank, I went up Gorky Street on the right-hand side. There, too, the smallpox announcements were posted everywhere. I glanced at them now and again as if I hoped to find something else written on them. Something other than the fact that a painter had brought a dreadful sickness with him on the plane from India.

What means had Vukmanović-Tempo used to get to Moscow, then?

The imposing edifice of the Hotel Moskva stood before me on the opposite side of the street. I scurried over the road and plunged into the foyer. It was completely quiet. In one corner, on the right, there was a stall selling foreign newspapers, particularly from the people's democracies and Western Communist parties.

'Have you got *Zëri i Popullit*?' I asked the salesgirl. 'From Albania,' I added, after a pause, to make myself clear.

When she held it out to me, I almost snatched it from her hand. I unfolded it in haste, scanning the headlines, the top lines first, then the middle ones, then the less prominent columns. Not a sign.

'Have you any back issues?'

She gave me a pile and I rifled through them at the same feverish speed. Still nothing.

I bought a dozen newspapers in a variety of languages and was about to sit down in an easy chair to go through them when I noticed that the salesgirl was looking at me suspiciously. I was irritated and went out. Although my fingers were freezing, I started to unfold the papers, sticking initially to making sense of the headlines on the front pages. Two or three people turned to stare at me with curiosity. I went back to the top of the pile. To begin with I just glanced at the front page of each, then at the back page, and then I went through the headlines on the inside pages, but nowhere did I see mention of Albania. How could such a thing have come to pass? I almost shouted. The thousands and millions of Roman and Cyrillic characters, weighing down both sides of my overcoat, like the lead type they were printed from, were deaf and blind. The newspapers I'd bought might as well have been in hieroglyphics. They taught me nothing.

Wandering around like a lost soul, I ended up in Red Square. Yet more posters were stuck on the front windows of the GUM department store. Dozens of them. Lenin's Mausoleum was closed. Perhaps it was the day when they aired it. Maybe it was closed because of the smallpox epidemic. Or perhaps they were taking measures to stop Lenin catching the disease.

A whirl of crazy ideas churned through my mind. All

of a sudden I remembered that Alla Grachova had invited me to lunch the next day at her parents' *dacha*. Amid the treacherous drabness Alla instantly appeared to me as an utterly delightful being.

Hundreds of people were pouring out of GUM, burdened not only by their everyday worries but also by the new anxiety from India. The microbe was present among them. It had smuggled itself unseen on who knew which handkerchief, lips or hair, and now it was turning the country upside down, as no visiting prime minister, president or emperor had ever done before. Two or three days previously, when it was still on its way, the city was at peace – as it had been a few weeks earlier when Vukmanović-Tempo had still been en route. It was the calm of yesterday and the day before when those innumerable bundles of deaf and blind newspapers had come into town.

I had wandered to the site where public executions were held in the old days. I tried to work out which side the prisoner had come from and where the executioner's ladder had been. There would have been a special roll of the drums. The sentence would have been solemnly recited with a declamatory tremolo, then the broad, half-Asiatic, half-European blade would have fallen.

I put up the collar of my overcoat against the wind blowing in from the Moskva River and began to walk back to Okhotny Ryad.

Sunday lunch at Alla Grachova's parents' *dacha* began in good humour but ended almost in tears. Alla told me that was usual in her family when vodka was on the table. Apart from her mother, her grandmother and her younger sister, Olya, there was also the uncle she had told me about, as well as two couples who were old friends. At the start we talked about smallpox; they presumed that quarantine would be imposed in due course. Alla's uncle, a ruddy, fat-faced man, bald and overweight, argued that there would be no quarantine, above all because it would make a bad impression on the political front. As he spoke he looked at me askance, as if I was among the supporters of quarantine.

'If it had been up to me,' he said, 'I'd have kept quiet about this disease. It's the sort of thing that's like manna from Heaven for our enemies. You'll see – they'll trumpet it all over the world, as if they've never had outbreaks of smallpox or any other calamity. Only they're clever, they are. They don't wash their dirty linen in public, but they keep their eyes on ours.'

He kept a sideways eye on me all the time he was holding forth. It was clear that at this table I stood for all that was foreign and hostile, from Western Europe to Standard Oil and the decadent bourgeoisie. Alla, who was surely well aware of his dislike of foreigners, kept contradicting him, and blushed with satisfaction every time when, in defending his position with excessive passion, he made some egregious blunder. When the others burst out laughing, Alla, who was sitting next to me, took the opportunity to whisper in my ear, 'I told you he was a right old Slavophile!'

'There's a real lack of gratitude towards the Soviet Union,' the uncle went on sourly. 'We spilled our blood for the peoples of Europe, we gave them the great gift of freedom, and they don't even bother to thank us!'

He looked as though he was staring at the piece of bread in front of me and I automatically drew my hand back from it.

Some of those round the table were paying attention to him, while others chatted to each other *sotto voce*.

'There is only one Communist Party in the world,' he resumed, without looking at me. 'One, not ten. There's a mother party and daughter parties, and people who say differently . . .'

I struggled to swallow the piece of meat that was in my mouth. Does he know something? I wondered.

Alla interrupted, 'Are there uncle parties as well?'

He glanced at her, disapproving. 'Stop it, Alla,' he grunted.

But his reproach had no effect on her. As she knew her uncle was really out to get at me, she seemed happy to have an opportunity to support me in an environment where I was entirely on my own, showing the warmth and sweetness of her nature.

In the course of the meal, despite Alla's interventions, her uncle got on my nerves. I hadn't yet opened my mouth, although I'd long been itching to retaliate. An opportunity arose, or so I thought, when someone alluded to Khrushchev.

'I've noticed that in recent weeks he's been referred to in the papers by pet names, like Nikitushka, Nikitinka, or Nikituchnok,' I said, in an excruciating accent, with the stress on all the wrong syllables. 'I know it's a Russian folk tradition, but don't you think it makes him sound a bit silly?'

While I was speaking the uncle stared hard at me, struggling to guess whether I was making fun of him or not.

When I'd finished, he replied, 'Contrary to the impression some people may have, the pet names show the people's affection for our Nikita Sergeyevich. Got that?' The beer glass he was holding was jumping around. 'Have you got that, *molodoy chelovek*, young man?' he repeated. 'Nobody would have thought of calling Stalin "Joseph", let alone "Yossifuchka"!'

There was evil in his eyes.

'Nikitushka, Nikitinka . . . That's how drunks talk,' said Alla.

I expected him to pounce on his niece, but all he did was look at her disapprovingly again. Apparently all his anger was being saved up for me.

He kept on coming out with unpleasant, double-edged observations, and I wavered between two reactions: to get up from the table and invent a pretext – a headache, for example – for taking my leave; or just to push off without a word of explanation. I would surely have taken the second option had not Alla's grandmother, who was, I thought, the only person present, apart from Alla, to have realised that I was the sole target of the old soak's bilious drivel, spat at him through clenched teeth, 'You should be ashamed of yourself, Andrey Timofeyich!'

The others didn't notice anything and carried on chatting among themselves. A young widow from a neighbouring *dacha* even seemed about to break into song. She tried out a few notes at low volume a couple of times, but didn't dare either to proceed or to give up, like a swimmer hovering at the lakeside.

Alla said no more. She was on the verge of tears, staring

scornfully at her uncle who continued relieving himself of spiteful remarks, but she had turned away from me. As for myself, I was trying to keep my temper by imagining those parts of Alla's body that especially attracted me: I was pretty sure that later on, when we were alone together, she would be more than usually comforting to compensate for her uncle's bile.

That was when something unexpected happened. The young widow from the nearby *dacha*, who had seemed about to burst into song, burst into tears instead. But it wasn't unalloyed weeping: it contained all the ingredients of the song she'd been ready to sing, including the words, which you could just about make out between her sobs.

'Come on, Rosa, pull yourself together,' two or three people urged, though their voices were also near to breaking.

Alla explained later that it happened quite often at her home. Most of the *dacha*s surrounding her mother's were allocated to the families of airmen who had been shot down during the defence of Moscow. It took almost nothing to turn a lunch party into a funeral wake. Her father had also been killed at the start of the German air raids on Moscow.

'Nina, do you remember when they called them out on red alert that night?' the young widow said, to Alla's mother. 'They'd just got home from a mission, but they had to go back on duty all the same. I had a sudden dark premonition . . .'

All of the women, those who were still widows and those who had remarried, began to reminisce about their long evenings and nights of waiting, their grim forebodings and their brief conversations over the garden fence.

Alla's father's plane had been surrounded by a squadron of Junkers and disappeared.

'Poor boy,' Alla's grandmother repeated, from time to time. 'Those vultures tore him to pieces. In the dark, all alone, up there, in the sky . . .'

All alone, in the dark . . . Those words hid something. They were like a bolted door in my way. I combed through my mind seeking desperately to resuscitate a memory. All *aloooone*, in the *daaaark*.

Suddenly it came to me. It was an old song someone had sung long ago at a wedding I'd attended:

> I set out for Ioannina
> In the dark, on my oooown
> Just me and black Haxhi
> In the dark, on my oooown

Every time I heard the words I heard them differently. Sometimes I thought it was 'just me and *arabaxhi* [the coachman]' and at other times it seemed more like 'just me and *arap Haxhi* [black Haxhi]', which I found even more sinister.

I shuddered. The thick of night, the road and black Haxhi, the servant. I couldn't remember the rest. I think the traveller was attacked by highwaymen:

> They cut me up with their knives
> In the dark, on my oooown

I thought there could not be a sadder song about lone-liness in the whole wide world.

'Nina, do you remember September the twelfth?' said the woman sitting next to her.

Wide-eyed and attentive, Alla's uncle was listening to the women's lively talk. The other men had taken on a look that was half guilty and half annoyed, presumably because it was not particularly pleasant for them to hear their wives talking with so much feeling about their first husbands.

As people were no longer paying any attention to us, Alla and I took the opportunity to slip away. Olya, Alla's younger sister, stuck to our heels.

'We'll all go for a walk in the forest together,' Alla told her. 'Only you're going to leave us alone for a minute. We've got something else to do first . . .'

Without waiting for a response from her sister, she took my hand and pulled me towards her bedroom . . .

The countryside, still half covered with snow, was silent. We'd been walking for more than an hour. Olya was with us part of the way and in front for the rest, because she liked to be the first to find the path we would take. A slim girl with delicate limbs and a supple neck, she had the same crystalline voice as her sister, Alla. From afar she pointed out a half-frozen pond, a derelict *izba*, and a half-rotted beam that someone had dragged out there, God knew why. We pretended to be interested in every-thing she told us, and she ran off happily to make new discoveries.

We came across a few uninhabited *dacha*s with their

shutters closed and, less frequently, an *izba*. Alla reckoned we were probably on the outskirts of a village.

'Hey!' Olya shouted from the distance. 'There's a cemetery!'

It was a village graveyard surrounded by a fence, or at least the remains of one. Most of the wooden crosses were broken or crooked, just as I had always imagined them from the masterpieces of Russian literature. By each grave there was a rudimentary bench made from two planks nailed to short stakes hammered into the ground. That was where the relatives of the deceased would sit when they came to the cemetery on Sundays or on the departed's name-day. Like the crosses, the wooden benches were black with age and rotting away. Nothing could have been sadder to see.

'There must be a church somewhere nearby,' Alla said. That was all that was missing from this deserted landscape: a village church with an Old Russian prayer book in the Old Slavonic that had seemed to be pursing me for a while. I suddenly felt sure I had gone past this cemetery last year. But maybe I was mistaken: the suburbs of Moscow are so similar to each other that you can easily mistake one for another. Or else I'd come here at the start of autumn when everything was golden and copper-coloured, streaked with the dust that reminded me of antiques shops.

I'd forgotten which station we'd got off at: all my memory retained was the magical gilding of the leaves contrasting with the black of the *izba*s, the carpet of dead leaves – the essence of autumn – and the birch trees with their spotted trunks, bare patches revealed by the peeling bark that were so bright and shiny that they reminded me of how village swells had once used mirrors to make spots of sunlight play on girls' windows.

I'd been with Stulpanc, Kurganov and a poet who worked in a publisher's office. We'd felt intoxicated as we'd tramped through what the glorious Russian autumn had turned to gold and laid on the ground but we couldn't understand why the two or three peasants standing on the thresholds of their *izba*s were glaring at us in such a sombre manner. We'd also seen three very aged women, one of them knitting; in their eyes shone the murky gleam of fear mixed with an unknowable measure of resignation. Puzzled by their attitude, we asked a few questions and learned that a nineteen-year-old girl had been stabbed to death in the area a month earlier. She was called Tonia Michelson and was certainly the prettiest young woman in the Moscow suburbs. She'd been killed by hooligans, not far from the suburban station, on the tra-a-a-cks . . . An aged country-woman wearing a headscarf (like all old Russian women) told us the story, her emotions and toothless gums turning her voice into a thin trickle of sound.

'They killed her for nothing, for nothing!' she said, and each 'for nothing' was like another stab to the heart.

Everything about her story was so raw and terrible that it made you want to double up to fill the pit it left in your stomach. The death of Tonia Michelson, a pretty girl of nineteen, seemed even more sinister told in a slow drawl from a toothless mouth.

Hooligans had come out from Moscow to see one of their mates. They'd been drinking, then played cards and decided that the loser's forfeit would be to bump off the last girl on the last train back to town. It was a vicious game that had been spreading in recent times. They gambled on the lives of complete strangers – the last customer at the supermarket, the first person to get off the trolleybus, or whoever was sitting in seat seventeen on row nineteen in a cinema.

'So it's like I told you, for nothing,' the old woman said, for the third time.

If she'd said 'for nothing' a fourth time, I think I would have screamed, 'Stop!'

The pain that the unknown Tonia Michelson had prompted was visible everywhere. It had managed to super-impose itself on the landscape, soiling it with bloodstains that would not vanish for at least a century. No geological upheaval could have left a greater mark on those parts than the grief of Tonia Michelson's death.

I wanted to tell Alla about it, but something stopped me, maybe just that we were not in that part of the Moscow suburbs. And, anyway, everything was covered with snow now – and snow seemed to require one to forget, at least until spring.

We went further into the thinning woods. Through the trees we could make out distant *izba*s on the forest edge. The birches were frozen, and their dormant shoots made bumps in the blistered bark that resembled infected pimples. The lighter streaks on their trunks now gave off only a dull gleam, as if the village swells' mirrors had suddenly been covered with dust.

We passed yet more empty *dacha*s: doors and shutters closed, verandas with blackened columns, leafless lilac bushes.

A few birds of a species I could not name sang plaintively all around.

'I think Stalin had a *dacha* a few miles from here, over Kuntsevo way,' Alla said.

'Stalin? A *dacha*?'

She nodded, happy to have aroused my curiosity. 'Yes, but it must have been abandoned long ago,' she added.

Olya, who was walking ahead of us, shouted something about a fox den. My mind was elsewhere and I paid her little attention.

'Over which way, exactly?'

Alla shrugged. 'I'm not too sure. Over there, I think.'

I stared for a minute towards where she was pointing. Bare branches broke up the huge grey lid of the winter sky. 'Is it a long way?' I thought I heard her eyelashes fluttering.

'Yes, quite a way . . . but I'm sure it's been closed up.'

I could see she was afraid that I would ask to go there. Maybe she was aware of the trees bending over us to enquire menacingly: 'So what do you want to get up to in that *dacha*?'

'I would have liked to see it,' I blurted out in the end.

'Oh, no!' It was almost a cry of fright. 'It's a long way from here, as I told you, and there's surely nobody there.'

'But that's exactly the way I want to see it, the way it is nowadays!' I said.

Alla blushed slightly. 'Anyway, I'm not sure . . .' she went on. 'Maybe I'm misinformed and the *dacha* is somewhere else.'

I noticed her face had got redder. I remembered when

I'd gone looking for Zog's villa at Dubulti. On that occasion it had been the girl I was with who was eager to find it.

Today it was the opposite.

It seemed that each of us was curious about the other's tyrant, but preferred to avoid his or her own.

'All right, have it your way,' I said.

The snow crunched under our boots. Olya was out ahead and once again trying to communicate something about a fox den.

'Apparently, he was frightening,' Alla said, after a while. 'He lived alone, like a hermit.'

She must have thought that talking about the *dacha* being shuttered and Stalin's asceticism would diminish my interest.

'Yes, that's what people say,' she repeated. 'He lived there on his own, like a hermit.'

'The Revolutionary Monk . . . that's the nickname his opponents used. Did you know that?'

She shrugged her shoulders as if she was lost for words.

One day, I can't remember where, I heard a drunk saying, 'Ah! What a wily fox our Nikitoushka is! Khrushchev is a revolutionary fox!'

Light was fading. Olya suggested we go back before nightfall, or we might lose our way.

'Yes, of course,' Alla said. 'Let's go home!'

On the walk back to the *dacha* the three of us made a game of finding the footprints we'd left in the snow on the way out.

I could feel the opening of a poem I'd heard recited long before making its way into my mind: 'What are these clouds forever flying past . . .?' After a moment I thought,

Yes, what are these girls who get mixed up with dead dictators . . .?

Fleetingly, the twilight splashed broad blue and black stripes over isolated *izba*s, hollowed-out tree trunks and the roofs of shuttered *dacha*s. Here and there trees shook their crowns and released handfuls of snow that sparkled one last time before disappearing in the half-light, which was gradually acquiring the shade of tarnished silver. We were leaving ever further behind us the murky forest where the Monk and the Fox would continue to watch each other in silence as on the eve of mortal combat.

When we reached Alla's parents' *dacha* I said it would be better if I carried on to the station without going indoors to take my leave of the others. She agreed.

The two sisters walked down to the station with me.

Looking out through the carriage window I saw that Alla's cheeks had gone crimson again. Olya must have been teasing her about me as I got on to the train. The innocent bites of a harmless insect.

They waved from the platform as the train set off. I felt worn out. I closed my eyes and sat there for a while, my mind blank. It was a few miles before I even began to hear what the other people in the carriage were saying. They were talking about smallpox.

'They rang twice!' Auntie Katya called from behind her counter, as she rummaged in her drawer for the piece of paper where she'd jotted down the caller's name. 'Ah, here it is. Yes, it was the Albanian Embassy. You have to call them back right away.'

What could the matter be? I wondered. A vision of a coffin lying thousands of miles away, in my home town, Gjirokastër, arose instantly in my mind. My mother's? My father's?

I pulled my address book out of my pocket and, with clumsy fingers, opened it at A: Antaeus, Alla, Albanian . . .

As I dialled the number a pit opened in my stomach.

'Hello, is that the embassy?' I asked in Albanian.

'Yes,' said a calm voice.

'You called,' I said, and gave my name.

'Correct. About a meeting this evening. You must be here at the embassy at six.'

Ice-cold sweat covered my brow. For a second, my eye caught Auntie Katya's suspicious glance.

The main reception room at the embassy was packed. Students, most of them men, were talking quietly to each other in groups of two or three. The three candelabra, which had been brought down a little lower than the last time I was there, or so I thought, cast a yellow glare. A large bronze-framed portrait of Enver Hoxha filled almost a whole wall. Nobody knew why we had been summoned with such haste.

At six, the counsellor came into the room. He was wearing a black suit, and perhaps it was the contrast of his white shirt that made his face seem paler than it had been the last time I had seen him.

With him was a man I had never seen before and who had probably just come in from Tirana.

The first few sentences of his speech, before he even got to the subject, told me that the rumours about a cooling between Albania and the Soviet Union were true. He stressed that relations between the two countries had been and remained good, but there were nonetheless internal and external forces intent on damaging them. So we students had to be vigilant not to provide pretexts for provocation from whatever quarter. To that end we were urged to limit, as far as we could, all relations with Muscovites for the time being. 'I mean especially young female Muscovites . . .' he added. My heart sank, not so much from what the counsellor had just said but from his having said it without a shadow of a smile. It was obvious that we all expected him to smile, as he had done on all earlier occasions when urging us to behave impeccably with Russian girls. Such sentences were always followed by a silence full of suggestive thoughts, such as: we're perfectly aware of what you get up to but don't make them pregnant . . . This time his face was stony. 'You will therefore have to stop dating them,' he went on, in what sounded to me like a weary voice. He spoke for two more minutes, stressing that relations between the two countries were good, telling us not to be unnecessarily alarmed, and especially not to mention any of this to anyone.

'Well, there you are, young men, that's why I called you all in,' he concluded smoothly. 'I don't think you need any further explanation. Have a good evening.'

It was one of the most peculiar meetings I ever had occasion to attend.

A rumour flew round that all the close relatives of the painter who had caught smallpox had fallen ill. The airport workers who had been on the site when the Air India flight had landed were all under close medical observation. People said that if there was a fatality beyond the painter's immediate circle, the whole of Moscow would be quarantined.

It was Saturday, when the most tiresome lectures were given. To amuse myself I watched people coming and going along Tverskoy. If the building had been set facing just slightly more towards the north I would have been able to see the statue of Pushkin and the doors of Central Cinema, where there was always a long queue. But I couldn't actually see either, and Tverskoy was as sad as any boulevard in winter.

The lectures were nearly over but I wasn't excited. The other students were steering clear of me. But that wasn't what irritated me most. What I found unbearable was that they spent their time staring at me but looked away as soon as our eyes met. It drove me mad, irrespective of whether they were venomous (as were Yuri Goncharov's and Ladonshchikov's) or sympathetic (such as Pogosian's, otherwise known as the 'Masses in Their Tens of Millions'). The 'Belarusian Virgins' looked at me with suspicion. Shogentsukov and the two Shotas did so with curiosity, and others, such as Stulpanc, Maskiavicius and a couple of generally unruffled Russians, with secret sympathy. The Karakums stared at me uninterruptedly, their faces expressing consternation; as for Kyuzengesh, he put on a show of indifference tinged with sadness. The only one who treated me normally, as before, was Antaeus. 'You'd have to be stupid not to see that you're going to be hit by a dreadful hurricane,' he'd told me, two days previously. 'Everyone thinks this cyclone will wipe you off the face of the earth, but I've been to your country and know the Balkan lands fairly well, and I know you'll stick it out . . .' That was the first time I did not feel I needed to question him further. Balkan lands, I said to myself, as if I had just rediscovered something forgotten and buried deeply inside me . . . And let nobody forget that we no longer live in an age when they can put our heads into that famous stone niche! 'Let it be a lesson': isn't that the motto? The red-brown walls of the Kremlin flashed before my mind's eye. Was it possible that someone was thinking of carving a new Niche of Shame in them? 'The time has come,' Antaeus went on. 'Your hour is nigh!'

'What do you mean?'

He looked at me pensively for a moment, then said, 'One day we talked about the *besa*, do you recall? Well, the time has come for the *besa* to confront perfidy.'

I couldn't take my eyes off him. I was waiting for him to add something to what he had just said. And then it came: 'We belong to the Homeric camp! Let nobody ever forget it!'

The Homeric camp! I said to myself. It was true. When Lida Snegina and I had started our affair I had amazed her by talking about the river that flows near to my home town. 'Lida,' I said, 'did you know I've swum in the Acheron, the river of the Underworld?'

She'd thought I was joking. 'But you're still alive,' she said teasingly. 'How did you manage to come back?'

Then I explained that I meant it seriously: one of the two notorious mythical rivers passed near to Gjirokastër and the last time I had been there on a trip with friends we'd come across hydrologists on strange boats made of blue plastic, struggling against the river's swells and eddies. We asked them what they were doing and they said they were surveying the river's flow for a planned hydroelectric installation. My story enchanted Lida.

Now she must be convinced that I really had crossed the Acheron and that I would never come back from *over there*.

The lecture came to an end. As we left the hall, Antaeus passed close by and whispered, 'Have you heard that Enver Hoxha is going to come to Moscow?'

'No.'

'Ah. So maybe the rumour is wrong.'

In the courtyard I noticed Ping smiling at me two or three times. What's got into him? I wondered. It was an insistent, glacial smile. Antaeus, who apparently noticed what the Chinese was doing and also my anxiety, leaned over my shoulder. 'It seems that once you've finished squabbling with all the countries in the socialist camp, you'll become China's darling . . .'

'Really? Honestly, I don't know a thing. All I do know . . .'

'Yes?'

The Chinese was still staring at me.

As I walked across the yard I suddenly felt a great wind coming over my right shoulder. 'Solitary demons that split open the sky!' I turned and saw the student from the Altai region. He'd lost weight and his eyes had mauve bags under them.

'Where have you been hiding?' I asked. 'I haven't seen you in ages!'

He said, 'Solitary demons of the socialist camp . . . '

'What's that supposed to mean?'

'That I messed up. I failed to copy you in any way. Demons that you are!'

He walked alongside me for a few paces. 'Is it true that German women have their opening set поперёк, horizontally, instead of vertically? Kurganov told me so. Oh! I would love to lose my virginity with a German woman like that . . .'

'You and your virginity can get lost!'

'Pardon me, demon. I forgot: you have other worries.'

At the railing I saw a familiar face.

'Sorry,' I said, 'but I think someone's waiting for me.'

It was Alla Grachova. She smiled at me. 'You see, I was waiting for you,' she said. 'Mama, Grandma, Olya and I are leaving for the *dacha* this afternoon. We're going to spend tonight and tomorrow out there—' She broke off. 'But what's the matter? Don't you feel well?'

'What?'

'You look washed out.'

'Actually, I've got a pain . . . in my ear. It's almost unbearable.'

'What a pity! Mama and Grandma told me to ask you to come along, and it made me so happy! Especially as my uncle won't be around.'

'Yes, it is a pity,' I said, in a positively icy tone. 'Please pass on my thanks. I'm truly sorry I can't come.'

She looked me up and down sadly. 'Are you in such a hurry?' she asked.

'Yes. Alla, I'm really sorry I can't accept. It was so nice at your family's place.'

'You weren't too bored last time?'

'No, not at all. Quite the opposite – you were wonderful . . .'

She was trying to smile but something stopped her.

We shook hands at the bus stop and parted. On the way back to the residence at Butyrsky Khutor, I remembered what Antaeus had said: 'Enver Hoxha is coming to Moscow.' The windows of the bus were frosted. I felt worn out. I wondered what such a midwinter journey might mean.

Quarantine was declared the following afternoon. Apparently someone not related to the painter had died of smallpox.

The city was too spread out for us to know exactly what was going on at the airports, railway stations and all other points of access to the capital. What affected us most was the closing of cinemas, theatres, skating rinks, art museums and department stores, and especially the ban on outsiders entering student boarding houses and hostels.

Dozens of young men and women had met up outside the entrance to the Gorky Institute in the faint hope that they would be allowed in to visit.

'Now you're really deprived,' said Dalya Eipsteks, a Jewish student from Vilnius, to Maskiavicius and me. 'Like it or not, you'll have to make do with us!'

Short and not pretty, but with a Parisian *je ne sais quoi* in her sly and lively eyes, Dalya peered at us through her spectacles.

'Humph,' Maskiavicius said crossly. After three months' strenuous courtship he'd at last persuaded one of his girl-friends to come to his room, and the quarantine had

ISMAIL KADARE

thwarted his plans. 'Humph! Sleeping with you would be like sleeping with Klara Zetkin!'

She came out with something in Lithuanian that Maskiavicius said meant 'boor', but I was sure it was much more vulgar than that.

'I really have no luck at all,' Maskiavicius moaned. 'I'm jinxed!'

At the porter's lodge a few couples were trying to bribe Auntie Katya. But they couldn't get in. What were Lida and Stulpanc up to? In what frozen parks were they trysting? In which cafés?

Maskiavicius continued to rant, half in Russian and half in Lithuanian, about the quarantine, India, Jawaharlal Nehru, that clown in a paper hat who looked more like a chef than a prime minister.

On the second day of quarantine, on the seven floors of the residence, there began what was only to be expected: a drinking bout. It was of a different kind from those that had come before: an understated, 'lugubrious and Eurasian' piss-up, as Dalya Eipsteks liked to say. That was probably because of the short supply of women. Their absence was noticeable everywhere, from the table and in the sound of voices, to quarrels and punch-ups. Now that girls could not be brought in because of the quarantine, we realised that their presence had previously served as a kind of permanent regulator. They'd cleaned the air, stopped it souring, prevented it rotting. Without them, words, gestures, songs and the rest quickly went downhill. Even the blood oozing from bruised noses seemed different, more viscous and blacker, without the vermilion hue that only the disturbing

· 174 ·

presence of womenfolk seemed able to confer on it in such circumstances.

For hours on end they drank, mumbled and had fights almost silently, sometimes in groups, sometimes alone, in bits of corridor lit by forty-watt bulbs made even dimmer by a coat of dust.

One night in one of these gloomy recesses I found myself face to face with Yuri Goncharov. He seemed to be barricaded behind the checkerboard pattern of his suit, as if he were standing behind the railings of hatred.

'What's your Enver Hoxha trying to do?' he hissed, through his teeth. 'He wouldn't be trying to play the smart Alec, would he? Ha-ha-ha!'

I was struck dumb. I was quite unable to focus my mind and formulate a riposte. My mouth felt as if it was opening into the void. A sharp stab of anger pierced my ribcage. Finally my mouth uttered mechanically a word that my brain did not control. Even before I heard myself say it I could see its effect reflected in Goncharov's face.

'Доносчик! Snitch!'

Goncharov flinched. A venomous grin of the kind that betrays extreme resentment spread across his face. He brought his hand up to his jaw as if he needed to hold it in place – it must have hurt him as much as, if not more than, it did me to get the word out. Then he said, 'Have you ever seen János Kádár's hands on television? Tell me, have you?'

I didn't answer.

'Ha-ha-ha! You really should take a look. Haven't you seen his fingers without nails?'

I still said nothing. Goncharov's face was close up to mine.

'He tried to scratch Russia's face with his nails. So we tore them out! Got that? Ha-ha-ha!'

Dorian Gray, I thought. I wanted to slash that picture with a knife! As it had the first time, my mouth opened automatically and repeated, 'Snitch!'

He burped out an 'Ooh', as if he was bringing up something from his stomach, and a second later neither he nor I was there.

The drinking continued. Afternoons were defiled with sausage, vodka and cheap tobacco. There was nothing but moaning and demands to be heard along the corridors. Now and again you could hear something like a drum beating slowly – that was Abdullakhanov banging his head against the wall again.

The sky was overcast. Even the snow had stopped falling. It seemed we would have to be content for ever more with the old snow that was heaped in piles on the pavements and at the roadside.

It was an afternoon at half mast that could have been from a page torn out of the last diary in the world. From the window of my room I looked out on the roofs of the housing blocks laid out one after another. I thought of the municipal apartments where, in the shared kitchens, neighbourly hatred had settled like a film on the blackened base of the cooking pots and on gas hobs covered with grease and grime.

And on top of all that, quarantine. In Russian the disease was called 'black pox', чёрная оспа. All over Moscow.

I was overcome with nostalgia to the point of paralysis; it swept away everything else. I burned with fever and the next minute I was shivering with cold. On my right shoulder, where they'd done a tattoo imitating the Asian sarcophagus of an Indian princess, I could feel a constant itch. That was where a weakened bacillus of the pox, isolated from its horde, had been tamed, overcome, trapped by civilisation, and was in the process of giving up the ghost.

Black pox, I repeated in my mind, unable to tear myself away from the window. The pox . . . How would I get through this evening, then the next evening, then the one after that? The dull, staccato thud of Abdullakhanov's cranium a short distance away no longer seemed quite so abnormal.

Lida! I am not as you imagine me! I suddenly thought. I'd leaned my head against the freezing windowpane, and in the condensation my breath made on it, I wrote her telephone number. Well, I thought, it's ruined between us, obliterated, as if by a wall of fog. Even if the quarantine were lifted as suddenly as it had been decreed, we two would be as before, two frozen, haunted shadows lost in a grey mist. Then as soon the airports reopened I would leave Russia with the other students from Albania on the first plane to Tirana. But I had promised her that, whatever happened, I would say farewell to her in person. I had given her my word . . . and I came from the country where nobody, wherever he may be on this earth or under it, goes back on their word.

The idea of calling her came to me quite calmly, as icily as everything else, without a flaw, brooking no objection. I paused before the phone booth in the corridor beneath the pale light of a forty-watt moon, just like in the ancient ballad. Then I almost said it aloud: The hour has come, Kostandin! Raise the lid of your tomb!

The dial rotated with difficulty as if it had been made of stone.

'Hello?'

Her voice came to me as through a filter of quarantine and mourning.

'Is that you, Lida?'

'. . .'

'Lida!'

'. . .'

'Hello! Lida, can you hear me? It's me . . .'

'Yes, sure,' she said faintly, almost inaudibly, 'but you . . .'

'Yes, it is really me – it was a misunderstanding, I know, I know . . . Hello?'

I could hear her gasping for breath.

'You . . . alive?'

'Of course I am, since I'm phoning you.'

She had used the formal вы to say 'you' but, strangely, it sounded natural to me.

'Lida . . . I . . .'

'Oh! Wait a minute . . .'

Time to regain her composure. She didn't say so, but I guessed. To be honest, I probably needed to readjust as much as she did. I heard her breathing awkwardly again. Then she said, 'I'm listening . . .'

I tried to speak very casually, inventing something about a misunderstanding, an air disaster that turned out to be not a catastrophe at all, just a scare, and so forth.

I picked up a note of doubt in the way she was breathing. At last I managed to say to her, 'Would you like us to get together at seven, at the usual place? Everything's so boring, these days.'

I was about to ask her whether the quarantine affected her quarter of the town as well, but then I remembered that the measure was universal.

'The usual place?' she asked. 'Where do you mean?'

'Well, at the Novoslobodskaya metro station, of course, by the old entrance, like we always used to.'

'Oh! Of course . . .'

Apparently she was still unsure, while I remained incapable of finding a way of proving to her from a distance that I was not a ghost.

'At seven?' she repeated.

'Yes.'

I'll have time to saddle my horse, I thought. That cold stone slab metamorphosed into a steed . . .

I waited for her as I used to at the old entrance to Novoslobodskaya metro station. From far away I saw her coming towards me in the crowd of pedestrians, with her blonde halo and her special way of walking, which seemed to have changed very slightly. You could see she was worried from the slight trembling in her knees, shoulders and neck.

I popped out from behind a pillar. 'Lida!'

I had realised she might be frightened by seeing me. As she told me on our walk, she had made up her mind not to let it show but, despite that, she jumped.

I smiled and gave her my hand. The station lighting made her seem paler, and she had slight bags under her eyes, which added to her charm yet made her seem more distant.

But it was she who said to me, still in the polite form of address, 'You're really pale. Are you ill?'

'Yes.'

We looked at each other. Her eyes were blank. Her sadness and fear seemed to have flowed to their edges, like the waters of a lake blown ashore.

Without saying anything, we forged a path through the throng of travellers coming and going at the metro exit. I got the impression a couple of times that she was glancing at my hair to see if there wasn't a trace of the earth of a grave on it. Good thing I'd told the legend of Kostandin and Doruntine only to that Latvian girl from Riga, last summer, at Dubulti, more than a century ago.

We went along Chekhov Street. At last, when we were abreast of the *Izvestia* building, she took my arm. World news was streaming in lights on the front, high up, at the level of the top floor. No mention of Albania. Her shoulder seemed to transmit a muffled sob to my own.

We'd crossed Pushkin Square and were on Gorky Street. The cafés were closed. We were galloping hazily across windows lit by the falling light of the late afternoon, just like the Quick and the Dead of the legend, sitting astride the same horse. I had a temperature. A side-effect of vaccination, most likely.

'Did you miss me?' she blurted out, without warning.

I jumped as though I'd been startled from sleep. She'd gone back to using the affectionate ты form of address, and on top of that the word 'missed' seemed pregnant with danger.

Ah, yes! I started to muse. You were missing me to the point of suffocation. Years of separation with no hope, no word, not even a carrier bird to bring me a note . . . It had been a desert, the desert of Yemen . . .

In a shop window I noticed packets of coffee labelled 'Yemen'. 'Far away in Arabia,' I said, 'there's a bridge, the Bridge of Mecca . . .'

She was listening to me, apparently enthralled.

> If she asks which woman he took for his wife
> Tell her, Lady Snegina from the land of ice

'Your hands are burning,' she said. 'Are you ill?'

'No, it must the vaccination.'

I wanted to ask her about Stulpanc, but he seemed as far away and as foreign as a bird.

The corners of the quarantine notices were beginning to peel off, as posters always do in winter.

'When I heard your voice on the phone I thought my heart was about to stop.'

'I understand,' I said. 'Nobody has yet rung up from the Other Side.'

She tried to laugh. 'Not even the pharaohs!'

I felt her hand tighten on my arm, which I could take for a sign of increasing intimacy or as the need to check there was a real arm and not just bones inside my jacket sleeve.

'Your letter . . .' I started to say.

'Oh! Did you get it, then?'

I'd have liked to say something more about Stulpanc, but he seemed to have drifted even further away. Her shoulder nudged mine once again as if to transmit a secret message.

'Let's go to your place,' she muttered, leaning even closer to me.

Her shoulders must have been red hot under her sweater. But her eyes remained as blank as ever.

> If she asks which horse he took as his mount
> Tell her it was the tram to Butyrsky Khutor

'But it's quarantined, like everywhere else. Haven't you heard?'

'Oh, yes, smallpox . . .'

Her sidelong glance scalded my forehead.

Better go to your place, I thought. It would feel more forgiving in her bedroom. She would undress slowly, and before we made love I would study each part of her body carefully, as if I wanted to find out what had changed during my absence.

I suddenly remembered the embassy's instructions about relationships with Russian girls. I thought the three yellow chandeliers of the reception room were about to come loose and fall right on top of me. I tried to cry out, 'What have I done?' and the chandeliers, as if they had heard my protest, began to hoist themselves back up, getting smaller and smaller until they were no bigger in my mind's eye than ladybirds. The same scenario repeated itself several times.

Well, what *had* I done? I felt a hot flush run through

my temples and my forehead. I'd been thoughtless enough to call her and try to resurrect an affair that was truly dead and buried. I'd done something really stupid and, what was more, to no purpose. Now I had to beat the retreat.

I consoled myself with the thought that I hadn't committed any great crime. I'd come out to see her just to keep my word.

'You look like death warmed up!' she said.

I didn't reply. We were now sauntering like a pair of lost souls amid the rushing crowd of Muscovites, with their heads snug in fur collars and hoods. I guessed all of them bore, like an emblem or a seal on the invitation to a macabre entertainment, the mark of the vaccination.

My temperature made my head throb. My mind was a muddle and I would not have been surprised if she'd asked me, 'Why is there soil in your hair?' I'd made her a promise, I said again to myself. I gave her my word last summer, and maybe well before that, a thousand years ago. In any case our night ride will soon be over, I thought, as we came towards Tverskoy Boulevard. I had to leave her, but I was unable to find the flimsiest reason to do so. Even if I could not tell her the actual truth, I still did not want to lie to her. The bottom line was that I had phoned her.

'You're not well,' she said. 'It's plain to see. Why did you come out?'

'I'd given you my word.'

Now I only had to shake the soil from my hair.

'I gave you my word,' I repeated, moving my head closer to her hair. 'I gave it to you long ago, in the age of the great ballads.'

She stared at me. It was clear that she thought I was delirious. I was tempted to say, 'You can't understand, your people have other ballads, other gods . . .'

She did not take her eyes off me. Suddenly before my mind's eye the current Soviet leadership appeared, looking as if they had been flattened by their fur hats, standing side by side on the podium in Red Square. They were visible only from the waist up, which made them seem even more squat and obese than they were. The stunted gods of the socialist camp! The Scythian steppe gods about to puff out their fearsome cheeks to blow my country off the face of the earth!

'You're boiling hot!' Lida said to me. 'You should have stayed indoors.'

She was right: I shouldn't have gone out. But I had given my word. All because of the old legend. I suddenly wondered why I hadn't been able to get it out of my mind for the last few months. Was it just by chance? Surely not.

The gods of the steppe were as stuck in my mind as if they had been glued to the top table at a meeting of the Presidium. With their fur bonnets, half-Asiatic cheeks and sly eyes. No, the resurgence of the Ballad of the Given Word was no mere coincidence. Called forth by treacherous times it had come back from the brink of extinction. By the climate of treachery I'd been aware of for months. It's cold in Russia, my friend. A treacherous climate . . . Who'd prompted those words in my mind?

Despite all of that, I was still trying to find a pretext for leaving her.

Lida, I thought, you'll not get a word of adieu out of me. It has to happen as it does in the ballad!

However much I thought about what I would say, I still could not take my eyes off her.

'Lida, I once told you, in a station, that, whatever comes to pass . . .'

'Yes?' she said, lips pursed.

We were outside the Gorky Institute. In the twilight its railings and windows looked even gloomier. The only light was a dim glow from a ground-floor porthole in the porter's lodge. I stood still, and as she waited for me to finish my sentence, I turned my head towards the Institute and said, 'Lida, you go on now, I have something to do here.'

I didn't say another word, I didn't tell her to wait for me and I didn't say adieu. Instead I opened the gate and went into the pitch-dark courtyard. I walked with my hands held out in front of me to avoid stumbling over the marble benches, pale blotches that, in the black of night, looked like tombstones. The gate at the other end of the garden that gave on to Malaya Bronnaya was locked but I had no trouble clambering over it.

I was on the other side, in the cold, dimly lit street, where a few pedestrians hurried past with their heads deep inside their fur collars.

As I walked on, I thought of her standing on Tverskoy Boulevard, facing the sombre railings around the Institute's garden and waiting in vain for me to come back from that undiscovered country, from whose bourn no traveller returns.

Tirana, 1962–1976

PRINCIPAL CHARACTERS
MENTIONED IN THE NOVEL

Other named characters are not necessarily fictional

ABDULLAKHANOV, student at the Gorky Institute, 1958–60.

AKHMADULINA, Bella Akhatovna, Russian poet and translator, 1937–2010. Suspended from her course at the Gorky Institute for opposing the persecution of Boris Pasternak. Between 1954 and 1960 she was the wife of the poet Yevgeny Yevtushenko. Now recognised as one of the greatest of modern Russian poets.

ARAGON, Louis, French poet, 1897–1982. Well-known in Russia because of his unwavering support of the Communist Party, Aragon was also a major figure in the surrealist movement and subsequently France's national poet of the Resistance. Husband of Elsa Triolet.

ARBUZOV, Aleksei Nikolaevich, Soviet playwright, 1908–1986.

BÜRGER, Gottfried August, German writer, 1747–1794. His romantic ballad 'Lenore' is based on a widespread folk legend of a man who rises from the dead to take his betrothed on a ride to the other world; it may also have been a source for Edgar Allan Poe's 'Leonore'.

CHUKOVSKY, Korney Ivanovich, Soviet translator and children's writer, 1882–1969. Author of much-loved nonsense verse and the doyen of the Soviet school of literary translation. He is reputed to be the only Soviet writer to have officially congratulated Boris Pasternak on winning the Nobel Prize.

DE RADA, Jeronim, Italo-Albanian writer, 1814–1903. A romantic nationalist from the Albanian-speaking community of southern Italy (the Arbëresh), de Rada wrote verse and prose in both Italian and Albanian, and is among the founding fathers of modern Albanian literature.

DRUZIN, Valery, editor of the literary magazine *Zvezda*, (1947–1957), deputy editor of *Literturnaya gazeta* (1957–1960), and professor at the Gorky Institute.

FADEYEV, Aleksandr Aleksandrovich, Russian writer, 1901–1956. Author of *The Young Guard* (1945), a novel of the heroic actions of a Komsomol unit during the Second World War. A fervent Stalinist and an alcoholic, Fadeyev committed suicide not long after Stalin's demise.

FEDIN, Konstantin Alexandrovich, Russian writer, 1892–1977, president of the Union of Soviet Writers from 1959.

GONCHAROV, Yuri, student at the Gorky Institute, 1958–1960.

KÁDÁR, János, Hungarian, politician, 1912–1989. Although a high-ranking official between 1945 and 1949, Kádár was arrested on trumped-up charges and brutally tortured by the secret police in 1950. Released from prison in 1954, after Stalin's death, Kádár emerged as the leader of the nation from 1956 and remained at the helm until 1988. He made Hungary the most Western-oriented and prosperous country in the Soviet sphere of influence.

KHARABAROV, Vanya, a young poet, friend of Yuri Pankratov. Both were expelled from the Gorky Institute and sent to Kazakhstan for their support of Pasternak; rehabilitated in 1960.

KUZNETSOV, Anatoly Vassilievich, Soviet writer, Kiev, 1929– London, 1979. Student at the Gorky Institute, 1958–1960. His novella *Continuation of a Legend* was published in the review *Yunost* in 1957 in a heavily censored version incorporating additional episodes that he later said 'were so outrageously cheerful that no reader would take them seriously'. He later published the momentous story of the wartime massacre of Jews at Babi Yar, and defected to Britain in 1968.

KYUZENGESH, Yu, student at the Gorky Institute, 1958–1960.

LADONSHCHIKOV, G.A., student at the Gorky Institute, 1958–1960.

MASKIAVICIUS, B.M., student at the Gorky Institute, 1958–1960.

MAYAKOVSKY, Vladimir Vladimirovich, Russian poet, 1893–1930. The greatest of all modernist poets in Russia and a man of wild passions, Mayakovsky was put under great pressure to conform once Stalin had consolidated his grip on power in 1929. By many accounts Mayakovsky killed himself to escape from such an intolerable prospect.

PANKRATOV, Yuri, see under KHARABAROV.

PASTERNAK, Boris Leonidovich, Russian poet, translator and novelist, 1890–1960. See introduction.

PAUSTOVSKY, Konstantin Georgevich, Russian novelist and playwright, 1892–1968.

PETROS, Antaeus, student at the Gorky Institute, 1958–1960.

POGOSIAN, A. A., student at the Gorky Institute, 1958–1960.

REUTSKY, Piotr I., student at the Gorky Institute, 1958–1960.

SERIOGIN, I. N., professor at the Gorky Institute.

SHAKENOV, Nutfulla, student at the Gorky Institute, 1958–1960.

SHOGENTSUKOV, A. O., student at the Gorky Institute, 1958–1960.

STULPANC, E.V., student at the Gorky Institute, 1958–1960.

TABUROKOV, P. I., student at the Gorky Institute, 1958–1960.

TRIOLET, Elsa Yurevna, 1896–1970. Sister of Lilya Brik, Mayakovsky's muse, and wife of Louis Aragon, Elsa Triolet was also a writer in her own name, in Russian and in French, and though naturalised French remained a stalwart supporter of the USSR.

TVARDOVSKY, Aleksandr Trifonovich, Soviet writer, 1910–1971. Author of *Vassily Tyorkin*, a part-humorous epic of an ordinary soldier's life through the Second World War. Tvardovsky was the editor of *Novy Mir*, the most prestigious literary journal of the time, from, 1950–1954 and again from 1958–1970. However, in 1954 Tvardovsky began working on a parodic sequel to his original Tyorkin tale, in which the hero visits Hell and finds there a distorted view of Soviet life. *Tyorkin Na Tom Svete* ('Tyorkin in the Other World') was not completed until 1963. It was published, but not viewed favourably by government and Party officials.

VUKMANOVIĆ-TEMPO, Svetozar, 1912–2000. Yugoslav partisan and Communist Party leader.

YERMILOV, Vladimir, 1904–1965, biographer of Chekhov, author of *Literature and The New Man* (1963).

YEVTUSHENKO, Yevgenyi Aleksandrovich, 1933– . Russian poet. Already famous for his poetry collection, *Zima Station* (1956), Yevtushenko was expelled from the Gorky Institute in 1957 for 'individualism' but was able to become a popular 'public poet' during the relatively liberal years of the Khrushchev era. Later on, his political position was seen as ambiguous, if not duplicitous. Now divides his time between the USA and Russia.

ZETKIN, Klara, German militant, 1857–1933. Famous for her left-wing convictions but not for her good looks.

ZHUKOVSKY, Vassilyi Andreyevich, Russian poet and translator, 1783–1852. Translated Bürger's 'Lenore' three times over, each time in a different way.

ZOG, Ahmet, Albanian politician, 1895–1961. Prime minister, then president (1925–1928), then self-proclaimed King of Albania (1928–1939). When Italy annexed Albania in 1939, Zog fled to Britain, and moved to Egypt after the Second World War. At the time this novel is set, Zog was living in France.

CANON▌▌GATE.tv

CHANNELLING GREAT CONTENT

WATCH

INTERVIEWS, TRAILERS, ANIMATIONS, READINGS, GIGS

LISTEN

AUDIO BOOKS, PODCASTS, MUSIC, PLAYLISTS

READ

CHAPTERS, EXCERPTS, SNEAK PEEKS, RECOMMENDATIONS

DISCOVER

BLOGS, EVENTS, NEWS, CREATIVE PARTNERS

SHOP

LIMITED EDITIONS, BUNDLES, SECRET SALES